ENGINERDS

Don't miss the next epic adventure!

Revenge of the EngiNerds

ENGINERDS

JARRETT LERNER

ALADDIN MAX

NEW YORK LONDON TORONTO SYDNEY NEW DELHI

For Danni

This book is a work of fiction. Any references to historical events, real people, or real places are used fictitiously. Other names, characters, places, and events are products of the author's imagination, and any resemblance to actual events or places or persons, living or dead, is entirely coincidental.

ALADDIN MAX
Simon & Schuster Children's Publishing Division
1230 Avenue of the Americas, New York, New York 10020
First Aladdin MAX edition February 2019
Text copyright © 2017 by Jarrett Lerner
Illustrations copyright © 2017 by Serge Seidlitz
Also available in an Aladdin hardcover edition.
All rights reserved, including the right of reproduction in whole or in part in any form.
ALADDIN and related logo are registered trademarks of Simon & Schuster, Inc.
ALADDIN MAX is a trademark of Simon & Schuster, Inc.
For information about special discounts for bulk purchases, please contact
Simon & Schuster Special Sales at 1-866-506-1949 or
business@simonandschuster.com.
The Simon & Schuster Speakers Bureau can bring authors to your live event.
For more information or to book an event contact the Simon & Schuster Speakers
Bureau at 1-866-248-3049 or visit our website at www.simonspeakers.com.
Cover designed by Karin Paprocki
Interior designed by Hilary Zarycky
The text of this book was set in Amasis.
Manufactured in the United States of America 0519 OFF
4 6 8 10 9 7 5 3
Library of Congress Control Number 2017931487
ISBN 978-1-4814-6872-5 (hc)
ISBN 978-1-4814-6871-8 (pbk)
ISBN 978-1-4814-6873-2 (eBook)

Preface

BEFORE WE GET STARTED, I JUST WANT TO
make one thing clear about the guys I hang out with.

I did not, do not, and will not ever endorse our "name" or "motto."

EngiNerds.

That's what we (excluding me) call ourselves.

And our motto?

"Because it's the nerds who are the engine of the world."

Now, if you'll excuse me—I have to go wash my mouth out. You see, I puke a little every time I have to recite that thing.

Anyway, there are a dozen or so of us, all kids who prefer to spend our lunch hours discussing science and technology rather than, say, talking about the guest list for what's-her-face's birthday party or who was spotted holding so-and-so's hand in the hallway. We usually meet in one of the science teachers' empty classrooms.

If for some reason none of them are available, we'll hang out in the hallway or gather in the gym. Basically, we do everything we can to avoid the cafeteria and the kids who eat their lunches *there*. And believe me—most of the EngiNerds have very good reasons for doing so. At one point or another every one of us has been picked on or pushed around or, worst of all, forced to help some kid complete a homework assignment or prepare for a test.

So we isolate ourselves and pick on and push around one another. Not physically, of course. All our picking on and pushing around is of the intellectual variety. I mean, you can't get a group of self-described nerds in the same room and *not* expect them to partake in a little friendly competition.

Or a *lot* of friendly competition.

And actually, now that I think about it, maybe it's not always exactly "friendly."

Which brings me to the guys.

I guess I could go through and list each of the EngiNerds' names, give their particular skills and interests, and then share one or two of their greatest hits—like the time Alan rigged up his parents' vacuum cleaner so it hovered a whole inch and a half above the ground, or the time Edsley gathered up two thousand straws and launched a spitball *over a building*.

I *could* do that. But honestly, that stuff deserves a book of its own. So instead I'll stick with the guys in this first part of our story, the four of us you need to know about in order to understand how we unleashed a horde of hungry—

Whoops.

I'm getting ahead of myself.

This is only the *preface*.

Let me try that again:

The four of us you need to know are me, Dan, Jerry Lin, and John Henry Knox.

Dan and I are best friends. *Have* been since the second grade, when the two of us teamed up during recess one day to make a fort out of some twigs and rocks and a few old T-shirts that had been sitting in the lost and found since we'd been in kindergarten. He's brilliant, Dan is, if a little serious. And unless he's in one of his gloomy or annoying moods, there's no one I'd rather have around.

I can't say the same for John Henry Knox. Well, I can admit he's also pretty smart. Okay: *really* smart. But he wastes all his brains (not to mention tons of his parents' money) studying clouds and measuring rain-fall and developing elaborate theories about how the world as we know it will be swept away by some "cata-strophic weather event" any day now. It doesn't help that he's super arrogant about it all too.

And Jerry—well, let's just say that if Jerry wasn't around to lighten things up a little (and supply us all with chocolate milk), I probably would've been driven nuts by John Henry Knox long ago.

Like how he—

But wait.

I'm getting ahead of myself again.

Maybe we should just get started.

You'll meet the guys soon enough, and then *you* can decide for yourself what to think about them.

1.

THERE'S A BOX ON MY FRONT PORCH.

It's big.

Brown.

Smooshed in at the corners and bruised along the sides.

It's for me.

How do I know?

Somebody wrote *KENNEDY* in thick black marker on the box's top.

Normally, I'd assume a random box on my front porch was from my grandpa. But this isn't my grandpa's handwriting. His is neat and clean, and this person's? It's a mess.

The only thing I can think is that maybe my grandpa disguised his handwriting. Maybe the

surprise of what's inside is so good that he didn't want me to know it was from him at first.

I start to wonder what the old guy might be up to— but then I remember that there's a big box on my porch with my name scrawled on top of it.

In other words: I'm too flipping excited to stand here and think about anything else. I want to open it up. I want to open it up NOW.

So I lug the box inside.

2.

WELL, I *TRY* TO LUG THE BOX INSIDE.

But the thing is heavy.

I'm talking crammed-full-of-lead-pipes heavy. Heavy like the box has been packed up with the pieces of a taken apart truck.

I try and try to pick it up. I try until my back starts screaming and my forehead fills with sweat.

Then I run around to the backyard and find a few sturdy sticks. I bring them back to the porch and wedge the tips of each of them under one side of the box. Because if I can use the sticks as a lever to get one end of the box just a little bit up into the air, then I can—

CRUNCH!

POP!

SNAP!

Before I can lift the box even half an inch, every one of the "sturdy" sticks breaks on me.

I pull my leg back and nearly give the box a kick.

Luckily, I stop my foot just before it connects with the cardboard. Because kicking a superheavy, possibly lead-pipe-filled box wouldn't do much. Much besides break all my toes, I mean.

So I go inside—boxless—and call up Dan.

3.

"DAN."

"Ken."

"Come over."

"No."

"Please?"

"Still no."

"Why not?"

"Because."

"Because . . ."

"Because I'm busy."

"With what?"

Dan hesitates half a second. Then he says:

"Stuff."

I sigh.

"You're watching that stupid show, aren't you?"

"What stupid show?" says Dan.

"*Ladybug* whatever. The one with all the insects. *The League of Ladybugs.*"

"So what if I am? I'm *not*—but so what if I was?"

"Dan," I say, "it's a show for kids. For *little* kids."

"Not true, Ken. That would be a false statement. False and probably founded on prejudicial assumptions."

I sigh again.

"Stop sighing," Dan says.

"Stop being ridiculous," I tell him.

"I'm not being ridiculous. I'm just stating the facts." He clears his throat. "First of all, the show is most definitely *not* stupid. It's educational. *And* entertaining. And if you ever gave it a chance, you'd see that each episode is carefully designed to appeal to both kids *and* adults, boys and girls and men and women too."

"Okay, okay," I say. "All right. Just put the thing on pause and come over."

"No."

"Dan—*listen*. There's a box on my porch. A mysterious box with my name scrawled across the top, and it's way too heavy for me to lift."

Dan's silent. Meaning, I know, that I've gotten him at least a little bit interested.

Eventually he says:

"What's in it?"

I can't keep from smiling. But I try to hide the happiness from my voice.

"I don't know, Dan. That's the thing. That's why I'm calling you. I wanna get the box inside before I unpack it. But it's too heavy for me to lift on my own."

More silence.

Then:

"What do you think it's got in it?"

"Well, I guess it could be anything."

"Even like . . . like a rocket?"

I highly doubt there's a rocket in the box. I'd bet all the money I've got stashed in the booby-trapped shoebox in my closet that the thing's not packed up with a rocket.

But Dan doesn't need to know this.

I don't need to shatter the guy's dreams.

So I say:

"Yeah. I guess, theoretically, it could be a rocket in there."

I can practically hear the gears of Dan's brain churning on the other end of the line.

"Can I leave in fifteen minutes?"

I check my watch.

It's 3:18.

And I just so happen to know that the stupid little kids' show that Dan's obsessed with runs from three o'clock to three thirty.

So I tell him fine—but not before sighing one last time.

4.

IT TAKES DAN HALF AN HOUR TO GET TO MY

house.

During that time I have a snack—popcorn dipped in heated-up peanut butter, in case you're curious. I also manage to scoot, shift, and shove the box all the way across my porch, right up to the front door.

That's around when Dan arrives.

"How are the ladybugs?" I say as he's walking up.

"Shut it."

I hold out my hand and Dan grabs it. Giving it a tug, he pulls me up off the box—I'd been sitting on it for the past couple minutes, trying to ignore the fact that it was there at all.

"So," he says, "how do we do this?"

I open the front door. Peer inside. Make sure my dog, Kitty, is nowhere in sight.

You see, Kitty's kind of an idiot.

I love him.

I really, really do.

But let's just say that I've encountered rocks with bigger brains than the pooch's.

Anyway, I don't see Kitty on the coffee table, under the couch, or slouched up against the radiator, and those are all his favorite living room nap spots. Meaning he's probably upstairs on my bed, or else in the kitchen licking the linoleum floor—that's the guy's main hobby.

Turning back to Dan, I say, "Coast is clear."

"I'll get this side," he says, and crouches down to get a grip on the box.

I do the same on the opposite side.

"One . . . ," I say.

"Two . . . ," he says.

Then we both say:

"THREE!"

5.

THERE'S A LOT OF GRUNTING AND A LITTLE

whining—all on Dan's part, I should say—but we finally get the box into the living room.

"Get the door, will you?" I say, and then head to the kitchen to grab us a couple glasses of water.

When I get back to the living room, Dan's just staring at the box. He's not saying anything, but I know exactly what's going on in his head. His brain might as well be hooked up to a loudspeaker.

Rocket. Rocket. Rocket. Rocket.

I hand him a glass of water, guzzle the other, and fish my house keys out of my pocket.

"You ready?"

"Ready," Dan says.

I run the jagged side of a key across the layer of tape that's keeping the top of the box closed. Then I pull back the flaps.

And it looks like I was right about that whole lead pipe thing.

Or almost right.

Because inside the box—there's metal. And countless pieces of the stuff too.

There are long, flat rectangles.

Small squares.

Trapezoids.

Round things.

Round things with holes in their centers.

Round things with long, straight rods sticking through the holes in their centers.

Round things with long, bendy rods sticking through—

Okay, you get the picture.

These are parts, of course. Individual pieces of a larger—and probably way awesomer—whole.

And looking at all those pieces—maybe two hundred in all—scattered about the living room carpet, I think, *Man oh man oh man oh man.*

I think that this might be Dan's lucky day.

I think:

This might really be a rocket.

BUT IT'S NOT A ROCKET.

This becomes obvious once we find the instruction manual, buried beneath a giant bag of screws and nails and nuts and bolts at the very bottom of the box.

The manual doesn't actually say what the thing is. There is, in fact, not a single word printed in the entire 163-page booklet. It's just diagrams and pictures and numbered instructions.

And even at the end, on the last page, there's no drawing or photo of the final product. Not a clue as to what this huge heap of metal is supposed to make.

Meaning there's only one thing to do:

Start building.

7.

"Who do you think it's from? Grandpa K.?"

"*Of course* it's from Grandpa K.," I tell him.

Grandpa K. is my dad's dad, and just in case you haven't put it together yet, he's pretty much the coolest person on earth, and also kind of my personal hero.

He's an engineer.

Or *was* an engineer.

Now he lives in this retirement community called Bright Horizons, where he mostly just sits around and moves a toothpick from one side of his mouth to the other.

Sometimes, he throws the toothpick away and replaces it with another one. Then he moves *that* toothpick from one side of his mouth to the other.

I spend every Saturday morning hanging out at my grandpa's, and it's usually the highlight of my week.

The only time it *isn't* the highlight is if Grandpa K. happened to have given me a gift that week. Because my grandpa's presents are the greatest—period. They're always the kind that require elaborate assemblies, and in my opinion, that's the best part.

Once he gave me eight identical toy train kits—the exact number I needed to wrap the tracks around the entire basement.

Another time he handed me a huge sack of miscellaneous materials and several pages of handwritten instructions showing me how I could construct a wind tunnel.

Why, you ask, would I want my own wind tunnel?

To which I say:

Why *wouldn't* I want my own wind tunnel?

Anyway, all I'm trying to say is that it really wasn't so weird for me to come home and find a big box of metal pieces and a booklet of cryptic instructions waiting for me on the front porch.

Wasn't so weird, at least, as long as the box and the booklet had actually come from my grandpa.

The handwriting on the box was wrong, like I said before. Grandpa K.'s is small and neat and precise,

because back in the day, before computers, engi-
neers had to have nice, readable handwriting. Which
meant my grandpa had written sloppy on purpose.

And that made sense, I guess.

It *had* to.

Because who *else* could the box have come from?

8.

DAN AND I WORK HARD FOR CLOSE TO AN

hour. By this point we're both sweating. Our T-shirts are clinging to our skin.

We take a break. Step back. Have a look.

Here's what we've so far got:

A large, three-dimensional trapezoid with a square plate missing from its middle and a long, thin, flexible rod sticking out of one side.

The pile of remaining pieces on the floor looks just as big as it did when we first started.

"Man," says Dan.

He doesn't say anything else.

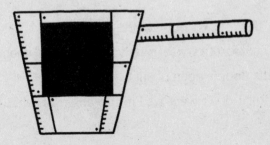

But he doesn't need to.

I hear him loud and clear.

Man—as in:

Well, this is quite the undertaking, isn't it?

Or as in:

I didn't expect it to take this *long.*

Or:

I could probably go for a spoonful of peanut butter right about now.

And man, do I agree.

I'm just about to head to the kitchen to get us some food and fresh glasses of water when a breeze blows in and sweeps across my back.

I shut my eyes.

I just stand there and enjoy it.

"This is nice," says Dan.

"It sure—"

My eyes pop open. Because I just realized something.

"Dan," I say, "you got the door, right?"

I could, of course, simply look over and check to see if the door is open or shut.

But I don't want to. I'm too afraid of what I might see.

◆ 22 ◆

"The door?"

"Yes," I say. "The *front* door. The one I asked you to shut."

"You didn't ask me to shut any door."

"I did, Dan. I most certainly did. I'm a hundred and ten percent positive."

"Well, how am I supposed to trust you about that when you don't even have a grasp of the basics of percentages?"

"Huh?"

"It's impossible," Dan says, "to have a hundred and ten percent of something, whether it's positivity or marbles or—"

I give Dan a shove so he'll shut up. Then I turn and look at the front door, which is open so wide a hippopotamus would have no problem squeezing through.

Or, you know, a not-so-intelligent dog.

9.

FIRST I SHUT THE DOOR.

Then I tell Dan not to move a muscle.

After that I check the downstairs and the upstairs, the basement and the attic and even the towel closet that I already know is way too small for a labradoodle to fit into.

But I'm desperate.

Unfortunately, that doesn't change the facts.

And the fact is:

Kitty is missing.

"Come on," I say once I get back down to the living room.

"Come on where?" Dan asks, though he's already started to follow me.

"To find the dog," I tell him.

"*Your* dog," he says.

"That *you* let out."

Dan starts to say something else. Something that

has to do with "property" and "responsibility" and a whole bunch of other stuff that I'm not really listening to.

But then—miracle of miracles—Dan shuts up. Just all of a sudden, in the middle of his sentence.

I'm so surprised that I turn around to look at him.

"Did you hear that?" he says.

"Hear what?" I ask him.

But before he can answer, the sound he heard comes again.

It's a deep, braying bark.

10.

DAN AND I TAKE OFF DOWN THE STREET,

calling out for my dog on the way.

"Don't, Kitty!" I shout. "Whatever you're doing, *don't!*"

There's a lady standing on the sidewalk up ahead. She's holding—not walking, mind you, but just holding, just carrying around—a tiny gray dog. She flaps her arm as we approach, apparently trying to get us to stop.

We do.

"Are you looking for a cat?" she asks.

"A dog," I tell her. "About this high"—I hold my hand up near my waist—"with curly, light brown hair. Answers to the name Kitty."

The woman frowns at me.

"Have you seen him?" I say.

"Your cat?"

"My *dog,*" I tell her—again.

"Named Kitty?"

"Named Kitty."

"Why?" she asks.

I glance down at the tiny gray puff of a dog in the crook of her arm.

"What's his name?"

"Christoph," the lady answers.

I blink at her.

I feel like my point has been made.

And so I set off again, Dan pounding the pavement behind me. A little ways up the street I spot Kitty: leaping into the air, snapping his jaws, howling, and just generally going crazy beneath the low branch of a large oak tree.

11.

I HURRY OVER AND CLIP KITTY'S LEASH TO

his collar. Then I try to calm him down.

But trying to calm Kitty down once he's gotten himself good and worked up is kind of like trying to stop a speeding train with nothing but a strand of cooked spaghetti. All you can do is give him what he's going crazy for or contain him until he tires himself out.

I'm trying to decide what our best option is when Dan says:

"It's a piece of pizza."

"What?"

Dan points up at the tree.

I follow his finger. And then I see it too. A cold, slightly old-looking piece of pizza. It's lying there atop the branch, perfectly balanced.

I look at Kitty. Watch him bark and lunge and leap a few times. And all of a sudden I feel terrible. I reassess everything I've ever thought about the dog.

Because all those times I've doubted his intelligence, maybe there was always a piece of pizza sitting there—metaphorically, I mean—just out of sight.

To make it up to Kitty, I decide to give him the pizza. I decide to let him eat the entire slice.

So I go over to the tree and give the branch a good shake.

The piece of pizza topples off and bounces onto the grass.

And then Kitty breaks my heart. Because he proves—for the fifty millionth time in his life—that he's got the brainpower of a wad of tissues.

He *doesn't* eat the pizza.

He rolls himself over and rubs his back against the slice until the cold sauce and congealed cheese is matted into his long, curly, previously clean hair.

12.

WE KEEP A HOSE IN THE BACKYARD ALL YEAR

round. Even in the wintertime you can find the long green rubber thing looped up, neatly stacked, and screwed into the spigot next to the grill.

This is not because my parents have a garden or because our lawn requires more than normal amounts of watering.

It's because of Kitty.

Because if Kitty isn't snoozing under the couch or licking the linoleum floor in the kitchen, you can be sure he's somewhere making a mess, and most of the dog's messes end up with him needing a thorough hosing off.

So Dan and I take the dog around back. Crank the knob above the spigot. Spray Kitty down.

"Hey," Dan says after spending a minute or two watching Kitty wag his tail and attempt to pin the jet of water under his paws.

I say:

"Hay is for stacking."

Dan smiles.

"You gotta bale it first."

"Right," I say.

"And it's also for building primitive dwellings."

"Well, *duh*," I say, smiling now myself.

Then Dan says:

"So you wanna call it a day, or what?"

"Why? *League of Ladybugs* on again?"

"No," Dan says.

Then, a second later:

"Well, yeah. Actually, it is. Encore showing at five o'clock. But that's *not* the reason."

"No?"

"No," Dan says again. "It's just that the thing inside, whatever it is, seems like it's gonna take another few hours—at least."

I nod. Because he's right. We've already spent about an hour working on it—and an *intense* hour, working *hard*—and we've barely made any progress.

"I've got this project thingy for tomorrow," says Dan, "and I've still got a ton to do on it."

I release the hose's trigger and then put the thing away.

"Just help me cart all those loose pieces up to my room, all right?"

Dan agrees and follows me back around to the front of the house. Then up the steps. Across the porch.

"After school tomorrow," he says, "we'll finish that bad boy up."

"Cool," I tell him. "But I can't promise I won't work on it some tonight."

"That's fair," Dan says. "It's your—"

He shuts up and stops about two steps into the house.

I do the same.

And the dog, too. Even Kitty hesitates in the doorway.

Briefly.

Then he's growling, barking, and hopping in a circle around the thing on the couch.

No, no—not the *thing*.

I know what it is.

It's . . .

Well, it appears to be a robot.

And those loose pieces that I needed help carting up to my room?

There isn't a single one in sight.

13.

"OH MY GOD. OH MY GOD. OH MY GOD. OH MY God."

This is Dan.

He's circling the couch along with Kitty now, studying the large, robotlike object from a distance.

I leave him there and quickly search the house for my dad or mom.

Who I know aren't here.

They're never home this early.

Neither of their cars is in the driveway.

And even if they *were* home, there's no way either one of them would've seen that heap of metal parts on the carpet and thought, *Hey, this looks cool. Why don't I finish putting it together?*

No, they probably would've called the dump and had someone come to cart the stuff away.

But what other explanation is there?

Who else could've finished building the robot that

is currently sitting on my living room couch?

I check the bedrooms and the bathrooms, the basement and the attic and even the towel closet that I already know is way too small for a parent to fit into.

Except for me, Dan, Kitty, and the robot, the house is empty.

I stop halfway down the stairs on my way back to the living room. I shut my eyes. Take a few deep breaths. Spend a second trying to wrap my head around what's just happened here.

Then I go back down to Dan.

He's stopped oh-my-God-ing. He's also stopped circling the couch. Now he's just standing there, staring, blinking, marveling at the robot.

He turns to me and says what I'm thinking. What I've already realized:

"Dude. It built itself."

14.

LOOKING AT THE FINAL PRODUCT, I SEE THAT

Dan and I had built the robot's torso—that tall, three-dimensional trapezoid with the square panel missing from its middle. And the bendy rod that we'd stuck into the socket on one side? That was an arm.

Or the beginning of an arm.

Now the rod—along with its counterpart on the torso's other side—has several cylinders on it, spaced out evenly from the robot's "shoulder" to its "wrist."

At the end of each wrist there's a clawlike thing. It's a simple design. Just a few long, hinged "fingers" branching off a rotating sphere at the rod's end.

Simple, yes—but I can tell just from looking at the hands that they'd be as capable as a human's.

Maybe even more so.

The legs are like the arms. Though longer. And instead of claws at the bottom, the legs have feet—long,

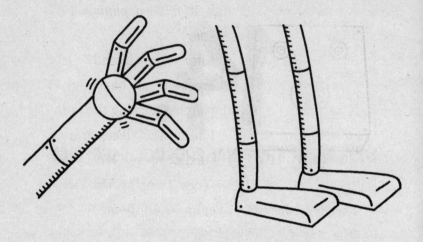

surprisingly thin flippers that are just a touch shinier than the rest of the robot's metal skin.

And then there's the head.

You probably want to know about the head.

It's square and sits atop a small cylindrical "neck." For eyes, the robot has two round pieces of plastic. These are tinted red, and I'm guessing they can light up. The mouth is also a round piece of plastic, but it's black and punched full of tiny holes, like a speaker. And last of all, poking up out of the robot's smooth, flat "scalp"—a small, clear light bulb. It looks like it was plucked from a strand of Christmas lights.

For several minutes Dan and I stand there and stare at the robot. We just take it in. Its presence. The fact

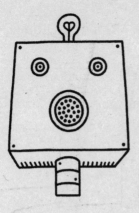

that it *finished putting itself together.*

Kitty has already lost interest—I can hear him in the kitchen, licking the floor.

Finally, Dan leans toward me and whispers, "*What now?*"

"*I don't know,*" I whisper back.

Then Dan whispers, "*Why are we whispering?*"

"*You started it,*" I remind him.

"*I know. It seemed appropriate.*"

"*Well, can we stop?*"

"*Sure.*"

I clear my throat.

Dan does the same.

"Should we . . . ?" I wonder aloud. "Should we talk to it?"

"I guess."

I take a step closer to the robot on the couch.

"Hello?"

The piece of tinted round plastic closest to me—the robot's right eye—flickers with a red light. Then the square head swivels to face me, and from out of the hole-punched plastic mouth comes a voice.

"Good MOR-ning," it says. "Good MOR-ning sun . . ."

"Son?" says Dan beside me.

"Sun . . . ," the robot says again. "Sun . . . sun . . . sun-SHINE."

Dan says:

"Oh."

15.

THE ROBOT'S VOICE IS A LOT LIKE YOU'D expect it to be.

Every syllable is sounded out separately.

The emphasis is all off.

It's empty of any kind of emotion.

And before and after and between words, there's nothing. Not the sound of breath moving in and out of nostrils or past lips—just a cold, creepy silence.

Yet Dan's absolutely right when he says:

"Cool."

Because this is most definitely cool.

This is beyond cool.

It's probably the coolest thing that has ever happened to me in my entire, twelve-year, not-exactly-amazing-but-also-not-so-bad life.

I take a step closer to the robot.

Then I say:

"My name's Kennedy."

"I AM *Greeeg*."

"Greg?" says Dan.

"*Greeeg*," says the robot.

"Greeeg?" I try.

The robot says:

"Yes that IS my . . ."

"Your . . ." Dan says.

"My NAME," the robot finishes.

"Well, um . . . ," I begin.

But what do you say to the robot who just built itself in your living room while you were out rescuing your not-so-bright dog before he could do anything too dumb?

Here's what I come up with:

"So that's pretty cool, huh? How you, you know—how you just built yourself on your own while we were gone?"

"Com-EST-ib-ulls."

I look at Dan.

He seems to be as confused as I am.

"What was that?" he asks the robot.

"Please FEED com-EST-ib-ulls."

"I think he's saying 'comestibles,'" I tell Dan.

"Com-EST-ib-ulls," confirms the robot.

"Okay," Dan says. Then: "What's a comestible again?"

"It's like food," I tell him.

Dan nods. Then, to the robot:

"What kind of comestibles do you want?"

"ALL com-EST-ib-ulls of lo-CAY-shun two-NINE-three-NINE-two-two-two-two-two . . ."

"Umm."

"Two . . ."

"Errr."

"Two-two-NINE."

Dan and I exchange a look.

"Maybe that means he's, like, *really* hungry," I suggest.

"Well," says Dan, "let's get the guy some food."

16.

DAN TACKLES THE SNACK CABINET WHILE I
go through the fridge. I push stuff aside and pop open
Tupperware containers, searching for and gathering
"comestibles" that might appeal to a robot.

Once we're done, Dan lays his things out on the
counter:

A jar of super chunky peanut butter.

Two carrot cake–flavored granola bars.

And a package of cheddar cheese–filled cracker
sandwiches.

I set out a jar of pickles, what's left of a pound
of sliced roast beef, and a squeeze bottle of spicy
mustard.

"Pickles and mustard?" Dan says. "Really?"

"*Spicy* mustard," I say.

He makes a face. "That's even worse."

"What are you talking about? How do you know
what a robot wants to eat?"

"I don't," says Dan. "But I know it's not going to be pickles and mustard."

"So you're saying you *do* know, then."

"No."

"*Yes.* You're saying—"

I shut up because I suddenly sense a presence behind us, like another person has just stepped into the room.

Dan must sense it too, because he turns around along with me.

Then we're both scrambling backward, crashing our elbows and hips into the countertop.

Also—I feel like this is an important detail to include—Dan shrieks.

He shrieks like a terrified ferret.

It's because the robot, Greeeg, is standing there no more than three feet behind us. Though how and when he got there, I don't know. It wasn't like Dan and I were making a ton of noise, and neither one of us heard a thing. Apparently, Greeeg can get about on his thin, flipperlike feet as silently as if he were stepping on pillows.

"You have ob-TAINED com-EST-ib-ulls," says Greeeg.

"Uh, yeah," I say, and hold a hand out to the spread on the counter. "Do you—I mean, is any of this good?"

"ALL com-EST-ib-ulls of lo-CAY-shun two-NINE-three-NINE-two-two-two-two-two-two-NINE."

"Right," I say. "Okay. Well, ah . . . help yourself."

The square panel in the middle of the robot's torso flips open like a little door. Then Greeeg glides toward the counter, so smoothly it's like he's hovering over the linoleum. In one hand-claw he grabs the pickle jar. In the other he takes the bottle of spicy mustard.

I'm fascinated and can't take my eyes off Greeeg. But I *can* lean over toward Dan and say, "See?"

He doesn't comment.

Probably because Greeeg has just placed the pickle jar and bottle of spicy mustard into the lower portion of his torso—his stomach, I guess—and is now reaching for the cracker sandwiches and the roast beef. He bends his arms to fit these past the little door too, plastic wrapping and all.

Dan says:

"Should we tell him the glass and plastic aren't part of the . . . the comestibles?"

I'm thinking we should, but before we get a chance, Greeeg has also gotten the peanut butter and the granola bars into his gut. And as soon as he has, he shuts the little door in his torso and pushes a tiny button beside it.

There's a sudden loud sound.

A churning and a crunching.

Like a trash compactor, sort of.

It ends as abruptly as it began and just a couple seconds after it started.

At which point Greeeg opens the little door to his stomach back up. It's totally empty in there.

"Please FEED com-EST-ib-ulls."

17.

WE FEED GREEEG EVERY LAST COMESTIBLE

in the snack cabinet.

    There are potato chips.

    Another jar of peanut butter.

    Rice cakes.

    Bags and bags of popcorn.

    A jar of roasted, salted cashews.

    Juice boxes.

    Pretzels.

    Hard candy.

    Soft candy.

    Neither-too-hard-nor-too-soft candy.

    Cookies.

    Animal crackers.

    Graham crackers.

    Regular old, plain, boring crackers.

    Marshmallows.

Packs and packs of gum.

Greeeg eats everything. And eats everything's packaging, too. Whether it's the nuts' glass jar, the juice's cardboard boxes, or the popcorn's plastic bagging, all of it goes through the little door and into the stomach-like compartment of the robot's torso.

And then every last bit of it disappears.

Greeeg shuts the little door. Pushes that tiny button. The trash compactor that he's got to have inside of him starts up, crunching and churning. And then . . .

And then his stomach's empty again.

It's like the greatest magic trick ever.

Dan and I watch it happen six, seven, eight times, and *still* we can't get enough.

And neither can Greeeg.

Every time he opens that little door and shows us an empty stomach, he says:

"Please FEED com-EST-ib-ulls."

One time, when Dan and I don't move fast enough to start packing the robot's stomach again, he even says:

"Please FEED com-EST-ib-ULLS ALL OF LO-CAY-SHUN TWO-NINE-THREE-NINE-TWO-TWO-TWO-TWO-TWO-TWO-NINE."

To be honest, it's kind of freaky.

But we keep feeding the guy. Even after we've cleaned out the snack cabinet.

Then we just move on to the fridge.

We give him blocks of cheese.

A half-pound bag of sliced ham.

One whole pound of sliced turkey.

Six apples.

Three pears.

A cucumber so long we actually have to snap it in half.

Carrots.

Lettuce.

Tomatoes.

Leftover chicken.

Cold pasta.

A jar of sauce that's so empty it's pretty much just a jar.

A carton of milk.

A container of orange juice.

Nine eggs.

And a bag of bread.

The only thing Greeeg *doesn't* eat?

Radishes.

I couldn't tell you why.

But there are a few loose ones rolling around in the fridge at the bottom of the vegetable drawer, and when I grab them and go to set them in the robot's gut atop a tangled heap of pasta, Greeeg goes:

"No, please not THOSE com-EST-ib-ulls."

I take the radishes back. Hold them up in front of the blinking pieces of plastic that are his eyes.

"These?"

"Corr-ECT," says Greeeg. Then: "YUCK."

It's weird. The only person I know who actively dislikes radishes is Dan.

I turn to him.

But he's not paying attention. He's across the kitchen, looking through some other cabinets.

"Dude," I say.

Dan turns.

"Greeeg doesn't like radishes."

Dan chuckles a little. But it's a fake, forced kind of laugh. I can tell that he doesn't really find it all that funny and/or strange that the robot who showed up on my front porch earlier this afternoon, the creature named Greeeg who consumes anything and everything, whether it's edible or not, also seems to detest radishes.

Which is weird in itself.

But I don't think much of it.

It's been a crazy afternoon.

Besides, Greeeg's getting antsy. He's not too happy that I've taken a break from filling up his stomach.

He says:

"FEED com-EST-ib-ULLS FEED PLEASE."

"Whoa," I say. "Easy, buddy. Don't blow a fuse."

I scrounge around in the fridge and find a shrunken, wrinkled half of what appears to be a zucchini. I hold it out toward Greeeg.

The robot grabs the gross, shriveled up nub and tosses it on top of all the other stuff in his gut. Then he shuts the door. Presses that tiny button. And the mysterious machinery inside of him gets crunching and churning. Again.

 18.

MOM STANDS IN FRONT OF THE OPEN FRIDGE

for three whole minutes before she says:

"Huh."

I'm at the table, pretending to do my homework. Dan left about an hour ago, saying he really had to get home to work on this project of his that was due tomorrow.

Before he left, he helped me get Greeeg upstairs and squeeze him under my bed. That, we decided, was the best place for him—my parents never have a reason to look under there, like they sometimes do my closet.

We had a quick chat with the robot before covering him up with my bedsheets, and he *seemed* to understand that he had to be quiet while my parents were around. And maybe you're thinking I'm a crazy person for trying to talk reason to a robot. But *you* try having a guy like Greeeg waltz into your life. You might start acting a little crazy too.

What I told the robot was that my mom and dad

might be mad and get rid of him if they found out that I had him—they'd done that with other gifts Grandpa K. had given me—and promised to feed him plenty more comestibles if he could pull this off.

Of course, I'd need to go and get some comestibles first.

Because the snack cabinet was totally empty.

And so was the fridge.

Which brings us back to the present moment, where my mom is still standing there, staring into the bare fridge, looking absolutely baffled, and I'm at the table, perspiring and getting pretty panicky.

Mom says it again:

"Huh."

"What's up?" I ask her as casually as I can.

"I just . . . I thought . . . Did we have a bunch of food in here this morning, or am I losing my mind?"

"Ha. Um, I—there's nothing in there?"

Mom turns back to the fridge.

"Nope."

She crouches down. Angles her head. Squints.

"Well, actually, nothing but a couple radishes."

"Hmm," I say. "That's strange."

Then I frown down at my open notebook. I pretend

I'm concentrating on an extremely challenging math problem. I pretend I'm concentrating so hard that I can't even hear the huge, record book–worthy sigh that comes pouring out of my mom.

But I do hear it.

And what I'm getting ready to hear next is something along the lines of:

Ken, what in the world did you do with an entire refrigerator's worth of food?

Or:

Ken, this is coming straight out of your allowance.

Or even:

Ken, go to your room and don't come out until 2039.

But what I actually hear is the fridge sucking shut. And then Mom says:

"I need a vacation."

A second later, a stack of take-out menus lands on the table beside my notebook.

"Looks like we're ordering," Mom says. "You pick."

With that, she heads upstairs to get changed.

Then *I* heave a sigh, this one of relief.

19.

WHENEVER MY PARENTS LET ME DECIDE
where to order dinner from, I choose General Noodles. It's Chinese food, and honestly, not all that good. The place is also notorious for messing up orders. It's not uncommon for them to swap one beef dish with another or to send over a carton of noodles when you clearly asked for rice. One time—I'm being serious—they delivered a sack of straight-up Italian food. We're talking ravioli and meatballs, eggplant Parmesan, and those little cheesy fried balls of rice, too. They even brought a few cannoli for dessert.

So why do I insist on ordering from General Noodles?

The chopsticks.

That's right.

Because no matter how badly they mess up your order, they always give you an absurd number of the things. Even if they bring you manicotti instead of moo shu pork, you can be sure they'll include a few dozen of the thin little paper envelope packages. It's like they think you're trying to feed a small army on twenty-five bucks' worth of food.

But you're probably wondering what I could possibly want with such a large quantity of mass-produced chopsticks.

Well, you see, the balsalike wood that your standard set of chopsticks is made of is thin and light and weak—but therefore flexible. And portable. And capable of being broken down and discarded or hidden in no more than a couple seconds.

Like one time last summer when Dan and I built a catapult out of nothing but chopsticks and a handful of rubber bands. The thing was great. We hung on to it for several weeks, just testing it out.

Then, on a superhot day in the middle of August, we set it up in Dan's neighbor's backyard, which is separated from his own backyard by a narrow strip of trees. We waited for Dan's older brother to wake up and open his window—then we began our assault.

We launched tennis balls and pieces of overripe fruit and even a couple water balloons up into the air and right into Dan's brother's bedroom, twisting the rubber bands based on the shape and weight of the to-be-launched object.

 55

The best part?

Every time a projectile sailed through his open window, Dan's brother rushed over and leaned outside. But of course he couldn't see who was attacking him. We were covered by the trees.

That didn't stop him from screaming at us though. From promising that he'd hunt us down and drag us up to his room to make us clean the smooshed peaches and pears off his walls and carpet.

But later on, when Dan's brother searched Dan's room, all he could find were a bunch of broken chopsticks and some rubber bands. And Dan's brother—not having gotten the same share of family intelligence as his little brother—couldn't see a powerful, finely calibrated catapult in that pile of "junk."

All of which is to say that I'm eating a beef and broccoli dish for dinner that I most certainly did not order. *But*, along with the soggy veggies and chewy chunks of meat, I got fifty-one sets of chopsticks.

I'm still unwrapping, splitting, and smoothing the splinters out of the things when my dad gets home.

He pauses just past the kitchen doorway. Sniffs the air. Says:

"What'd we get?"

"The General's," I tell him.

He says:

"Gross."

But he grabs a fork and a container of something from the counter and brings it upstairs with him, taking a few bites along the way.

20.

I CHECK ON GREEEG BEFORE GOING TO BED.

He's still there. Right where Dan and I put him. Laid out on the carpet beneath my bed, his flat face nearly pressed up against my mattress. I can tell the guy hasn't moved so much as an inch. I guess we gave him enough to eat.

I floss. Brush my teeth. Stand there for a while in the bathroom doing nothing but wondering what I might be able to do with some dental floss and 102 thin, tapered lengths of balsalike wood.

Finally, I head to bed.

I have some trouble falling asleep. Every two minutes I lean down and check to make sure Greeeg's still there. He always is, and after an hour or so of checking, I finally pass out.

I dream.

Not so surprisingly, I dream about Greeeg.

We're on a stage. I'm giving a presentation, telling a

big audience about my world revolutionizing robot.

But then, when I go to *show* the eager crowd just how Greeeg's going to revolutionize the world . . .

The robot won't do a thing.

All he does is say:

"Please more com-EST-ib-ulls PLEASE FEED."

I jerk awake. Blink at the thick darkness that's hunkered down in my bedroom.

As soon as my eyes adjust enough to see a bit, I decide to check under my bed for Greeeg again.

And thank God I do.

Because the robot—he's gone.

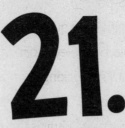

21.

GREEEG'S IN THE KITCHEN. I TURN THE
corner just as he's sticking the containers of leftover
Chinese food into the little door of his torso. It makes my
head spin just thinking about how much food the guy's
already got packed inside of him. And he's *still* hungry.

"*Greeeg*," I hiss.

The robot pauses for a second.

"I AM *Greeeg*," he says.

Then he goes back to filling up his stomach.

"Listen," I tell him. "You can't . . ." I don't know what
to call it at first, all that crunching and churning. Then
I realize what it most closely resembles and can only
hope that Greeeg understands what I'm saying. "You
can't do any digesting right now, okay?"

"Di-GES-ting," says Greeeg. "AF-ter FEED-ing
comes di-GES-ting."

"Right," I say, feeling relieved. "*That.* You can't do it
right now. It's too loud. You'll wake up my parents."

"*Greeeg* can DIS-pose."

He doesn't say it like a question, but I can tell it is one by the way the robot's eyes blink patiently.

And here's what I'm thinking:

How bad can Greeeg's "disposal" process be?

When he crunches and churns the food and its glass or plastic or paper packaging, it all disappears. Where it goes, I don't know. But it definitely *goes*.

I'm thinking the guy will open a vent and let out some compressed air. Or maybe there'll be a valve and some steam. Either way, it won't be too noisy.

So I shrug.

I say:

"Sure, Greeeg. Dispose away."

A small panel in the upside-down trapezoid that is the robot's pelvis slides aside, and out shoots a tiny brown-black cube. I barely see the thing. It soars across the kitchen in about point-zero-six seconds, then crashes through the window above the sink.

The shattering glass is as loud as a gunshot.

Kitty instantly starts to squeal.

And based on the series of sounds that follow, I can tell that the dog is now trying to squirm out from under the couch.

Two seconds later, I hear my dad call out. "What in the heck was that?!"

And then my mom: "Ken?!"

Greeeg, meanwhile, has this to say: "Dis-POSE-al COM-*pleeet.*"

22.

FOR A SECOND. ALL I CAN DO IS STARE AT

Greeeg in confusion. Also, I admit, a little fear. After all, the guy just farted a speeding bullet. What if I had happened to be standing right behind him?

I don't get a chance to think this possibility through. I can hear my parents clambering down the stairs, and I know that if (a) I want to keep them from "disposing" of Greeeg and (b) I want to avoid being grounded until I turn twenty-eight, I'd better get the robot out of sight—*fast*.

So I grab Greeeg, drag him across the kitchen, open the cabinet of pots and pans, and shove him inside. He goes in willingly enough, retracting and bending his flexible limbs in order to squeeze his body beside and around and over the things.

I get the cabinet door shut just as my parents are rounding the corner into the kitchen.

"*Ken*," my mom says.

She sounds relieved and confused and also maybe a little angry.

Dad's looking from me to the shattered glass above the sink. Finally, his gaze settles back on me.

"Explain."

At first all I can do is stammer.

"Um, ah," I say.

Then I say, "Ah, um."

I think I throw in a "well" and a "so," too. You know, just for some variety.

When at last I remember how to speak, I say:

"I was just standing here, just—"

"Why?" my dad interrupts. "It's"—he glances at the clock on the oven—"two thirty-three in the morning."

"I . . . water," I say. "I wanted a glass of water. And then the window—it just—it just all of a sudden—"

I'm interrupted again.

But not, this time, by my dad.

This time it's by a series of loud, bright crashes. The sounds of pots and pans spilling over one another.

23.

BOTH MOM AND DAD STOMP ACROSS THE

kitchen toward the cabinet to investigate.

Meaning I'm done for. My parents are going to open that cabinet, meet Greeeg, put two and two together, and lock me in my bedroom for the foreseeable future.

But one of us—either me or Greeeg—must have some kind of guardian angel looking out for us.

That, or the universe was just feeling bored and generous at 2:33 on a Friday morning.

Because before Mom and Dad can reach the cabinet, there's yet another crash.

This one comes from outside.

And along with it, half a second after that crash of a thunderclap rips apart the sky, little white pellets—dozens and dozens of them—come streaming through the window.

They bounce on the countertop and gather in the sink. A few—and then, quickly, a few more—make it down to the floor and roll and slide their way across the linoleum toward us.

Ice.

That's what it is.

Hail.

Mom and Dad and I all seem to recognize this at the same time. And as soon as we do, we all spring into action. The kitchen becomes a swirl of frantic activity.

I go straight to the drawer beside the sink and get a roll of duct tape.

By the time I turn back around, Mom's got a big black trash bag in her arms.

Dad hops up onto the counter and waves me and Mom over. He grabs the trash bag, spreads it out, and holds it over the damaged window.

I tug a length of tape from the roll. Tear it free with my teeth. Fix it to the frame of the trash bag–covered window and then tug again at the roll.

Within a minute we've got the bag taped in place. We keep taping though, especially because the hail is hammering so hard at the black plastic.

But it won't break through. It *can't.* As I learned from Grandpa K., there aren't many problems that can't be solved with a roll of duct tape.

Once we're done, Dad climbs down off the counter.

Mom goes into the next room, helps Kitty out from under the couch, and brings him in to help clean up the hail-littered floor.

Luckily, Greeeg stays quiet throughout the whole ordeal. I guess he's tuckered out after his disposal. And my parents—they must still be half-asleep, because they seem to think the crash in the cabinet was some-how related to the hailstorm. They don't say a thing about it. They make sure Kitty's lapped up every last ice-bit off the floor, then they head upstairs.

I wait until I hear their bedroom door close, and only then do I go and get Greeeg.

He's still in the cabinet, his limbs all contorted, looped through the handle of a pasta pot or holding up a frying pan. He's got a strainer atop his square head, like an ugly hat.

I help him out as carefully and quietly as I can, then go to bring him back upstairs.

At the last second though, I grab that roll of duct tape. And safe again in my bedroom, I tear two pieces free. I place one over the speaker that is Greeeg's mouth. The other I put over the panel on the back of that upside-down trapezoid—you know, his food-cube-firing butt.

24.

I DON'T GET ANOTHER WINK OF SLEEP THAT

night. I've got a billion questions bouncing around my head—plus an apparently never-not-hungry and potentially kind of dangerous robot lying just under my bed.

The questions in my head are all about him.

Greeeg.

Where is he from?

What else can he do?

Is he the world's most amazing gadget—or nothing but a one-trick nuisance?

I mean, if all he can do is fit the contents of a refrigerator in his stomach, squash it down until it's the size of an ice cube, then shoot said cube out of his backside fast enough to shatter a kitchen window, why would anyone have bothered to build him?

I know my grandpa will have the answers to all these questions and that I can ask him tomorrow during my regular Saturday morning visit.

But that would involve waiting a whole twenty-four hours.

And to that I say:

Thanks, but no thanks.

By the time my alarm clock goes off though, I still haven't gotten any closer to answering even a single one of my questions. And honestly, a part of me wants to fake sick just to stay home with Greeeg and keep at it. But another part of me wants to talk to Dan about what the robot did in the middle of the night. And yet *another* part of me—the biggest, I'll admit—just can't wait to see the look on John Henry Knox's face when I tell him and the rest of the EngiNerds that I've got my very own walking, talking, comestible-devouring robot.

I sit down and have a talk with Greeeg, man-to-robot, before I leave for the day. I tell him that he has to stay put. That I'll give him some more comestibles when I get home, but that until then, he can't budge from under my bed.

I'm not sure if he understands or agrees.

When I pull the duct tape off his mouth, all he says is, "I AM *Greeeg.*"

Just in case, I grab some more tape and fix Greeeg's

right arm to the frame of my bed. Then I hurry out of the house so I don't miss the bus.

At school, I find Dan waiting for me at my locker.

"How is he?" he says. "How's Greg?"

"*Greeeg,*" I correct him.

"Greeeg," he says. "Whatever. How is he?"

"How is he . . . ," I say. "Hmmm. Do you mean before or after he tried to kill me with a fart-bullet?"

Dan just blinks at me.

So I tell him about the little poop-colored cube that came firing out from Greeeg's backside in the middle of the night.

"But . . . ," Dan says, "that's not . . ."

He looks puzzled. Which is what I'd been expecting. But he also looks more than a little concerned. Scared, even.

I don't know why. But I try to calm him down.

"Listen," I tell him. "I don't know why the guy's got a cannon in his butt. I'm just giving you the facts."

Dan doesn't seem all that satisfied with this. He's staring at a patch of empty air in the middle of the hallway.

That's when the day's first bell rings.

I slap my hand down on Dan's shoulder.

"Look, man. It's Friday. Let's just try and get through the day without driving ourselves nuts. Greeeg's not going anywhere. I've got him duct taped up under my bed. Come over after school, and then we'll have the whole weekend to figure it all out."

Dan doesn't say whether he will or won't come over. He just goes on staring at that big hunk of nothing hanging there in the hallway.

I give him a shake.

"I'll see you at lunch," I say. "Now, hurry up. You're gonna be late."

25.

WHEN LUNCHTIME FINALLY COMES, I'M ONE
of the first EngiNerds to get to the empty science room
where we usually meet. It was a long morning, and I'm
just about bursting with my news about Greeeg. But I
keep a lid on it, because John Henry Knox is late.

I ask around to make sure he's in school that day,
and one of the guys tells me he just saw him down in
the computer lab, and that he's freaking out about that
hailstorm from the night before.

"Hailstorm?" says Dan beside me. "What hailstorm?"

"Last night," I tell him. "Or, actually, super early this
morning. Right around the time Greeeg tried to take
me out with his turd-missile."

Dan holds up his tuna sandwich.

"I'm trying to eat here."

I hold up my bagel.

"Me too."

Dan takes another bite of his sandwich. He chews it thoughtfully for a second, then swallows and says:

"I know you don't like him, that he gets on your nerves. . . ."

There's no need for him to tell me that he's talking about John Henry Knox. I already know.

"But what?" I say.

"He makes some good points," Dan tells me. "I mean, if you look at his analysis of weather patterns, if you actually listen to his theory about global—"

I hold up a hand to stop Dan before he can subject me to any more of John Henry Knox's meteorological mumbo jumbo. I know I'll get more than enough of it when the kid himself arrives.

And speak of the devil, not two seconds later John Henry Knox comes barreling into the room.

He's got a laptop under one arm and a bunch of scribbled on papers under the other. He plops everything down on an empty desk and then right away starts lecturing at us.

"The storm was not forecast by any of the major national weather services, nor any local meteorologists. It began slowly, with approximately twenty-six individual pieces of precipitation falling within a randomly selected ten-foot-by-ten-foot patch of pavement per minute for three minutes and eleven seconds. Then, in a manner that could only be described as 'abrupt,' the storm grew in strength. It quickly became impossible to get any accurate readings regarding the rate of precipitation."

He pauses to take a breath, and before he can start up again I say, "Hey. I got a reading."

John Henry Knox whips his head toward me. Narrows his eyes.

I can tell he's skeptical. Like he knows I might just be messing with him. Setting him up for disappointment.

But he's too curious not to ask.

Hesitantly, he says:

"Y-you did?"

I nod. Take a sip of my ginger ale. Tell him:

"Sure. A buttload of pieces of falling ice every point-two-eight-nine seconds."

John Henry Knox scowls at me.

"That," he says, "is *not* a scientifically sound state-ment."

"Maybe not," I admit.

And then I shrug. Because John Henry Knox is *not* a fan of shrugs. They're too vague and unscientific. They always make his lips curl up in disgust.

"But," I say, "I've got something way more exciting than *this* to talk about."

John Henry Knox chuckles.

"Way more exciting than a potentially apocalyptic megastorm?"

I grin.

I nod.

I tell him:

"I got a robot."

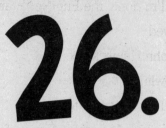

EVERY ONE OF THE ENGINERDS LOOKS UP

from his lunch and zeros in on me.

Across from me, Jerry accidentally makes a fist and sends a stream of chocolate milk squirting up into the air. The liquid hits the carpet with a quick series of splats.

Then there's silence.

Dan, not me, is the one to break it.

"It's true," he says.

John Henry Knox scowls again and says:

"What do you mean, a 'robot.' That's one of the least descriptive words in the English language."

This, of course, isn't true.

But John Henry Knox is angry—and probably a little jealous, too—and when he's all worked up like this, he doesn't always make the most "scientifically sound" statements.

So I tell him and the rest of the EngiNerds all about Greeeg, not leaving out a single detail.

By the time I'm done, the EngiNerds are all staring at me slack-jawed.

Except for John Henry Knox.

He's still scowling.

Once again, Dan's the first to speak.

"I've been thinking," he says. "What if . . . what if the robot was devised as some sort of food storage system."

"Storage?" I say, shaking my head. "But he only *stored* the food for a few hours. Then he fired it across my kitchen at ninety miles an hour. Unless . . . ," I add, a thought just then floating into my head. "Unless he wasn't *supposed* to fire the little food-cube thing. Maybe he was just supposed to, I don't know, plop it down or something?"

Beside me, Dan starts grinning. I don't know why. He looks kind of crazy though.

"Tell me where you got it."

It's John Henry Knox, staring at me with a mix of determination and longing in his eyes.

"I already did," I tell him. "The box was just sitting on my porch when I got home yesterday."

"But who put it on your porch?"

I don't see any harm in telling him, so I do.

"My grandpa. Or, probably, more like someone did it *for* my grandpa. There's no way he could've lugged that thing around himself."

John Henry Knox says:

"Well, where did he get it?"

"How should I know? It was a present."

"Ask him."

"No."

"Then I will myself."

"Oh, right," I say. "Because you know where he lives."

John Henry Knox's scowl comes back. And with a vengeance, too. His face looks like a dried, shriveled-up prune.

He glares at me like that for several seconds. Then he reaches for his laptop and starts to hammer away at the keyboard.

I can only assume that he's trying to hunt down my gift-giving grandpa.

But I really couldn't care less. Because I've got the one-of-a-kind robot in my bedroom. And in just a few short hours I'll be back there with him, nothing but a gloriously empty weekend stretching out ahead of us.

27.

THE AFTERNOON IS EVEN HARDER TO GET

through than the morning. For some reason, I keep wondering whether I should've used a little more duct tape on Greeeg's arm and keep imagining what he might do if he managed to get himself free.

By the time the day's final bell rings, and I go to grab Dan at his locker, I'm desperate to get home to Greeeg.

But not so desperate that I can't take a second to complain to him about John Henry Knox.

"Can you believe that kid?" I say as soon as I get over to Dan.

"What kid?" he says, dumping a bunch of books and papers into his locker.

"John Henry Knox. He's gonna try and kidnap my grandpa or something."

"No he's not," Dan says. "He's just . . . he gets excited about stuff. That's not a bad thing."

"It can be. If it's bad stuff you're getting excited about, it can be a *terrible* thing."

To bolster my point, I give Dan the first example that springs to mind:

"The Aztecs," I tell him. "They were really excited about human sacrifice. And look what it did for them."

Dan, now loading up his backpack, stops.

"What'd it do for them?"

I shake my head, like it's obvious.

"Have you ever met an Aztec? Ever seen one around?"

Dan sighs.

"That's the stupidest thing I've ever heard."

"Oh really? It is? Stupider than someone having a fit about above-average amounts of rainfall, concluding that the end of the world is upon us, and spending thousands of his parents' dollars to figure out how to efficiently stockpile food and supplies?"

Dan goes back to loading his backpack.

"What?" I ask him, since I can tell he's aggravated with me.

"I don't get why you're so hard on the guy," Dan says.

"I'm not hard on him."

"Yeah, you are."

"Not any harder than he is on me. And you wanna

know what *I* don't get? I don't get why *you* cut the guy so much slack. He thinks he's better than everyone, Dan. I promise you—he thinks he's *way* smarter than you."

Dan slams his locker shut.

"He *is*, Ken. The kid's a genius. Have you ever sat down and read some of what he's been writing? Have you ever taken the time to look—to really look—at his calculations? It's amazing stuff."

"Whatever, man," I say. "Let's just go. The buses are probably here already. And Greeeg's gotta be starving by now."

I turn around to go, but stop when I realize that Dan's not following me.

"Come on," I tell him.

But he still doesn't come. And now, instead of angry, he looks sort of nervous.

"Let's *go*," I say.

"I—I can't."

"What? Why not?"

"I've . . . got that project."

I think back to yesterday.

"The one you said was due *today*?"

Dan starts to gnaw on his lip. Which he does only

when he's nervous. Or when he's lying. Or when he's nervous about lying.

"No, it's . . . ," he says.

"It's what?" I ask him.

"We—we got an extension," Dan says.

Then he goes back to chewing his lip.

I can tell he's not going to budge. So I just say, "Whatever," and head to the buses by myself.

28.

I HAVE TO GET OFF THE BUS A COUPLE STOPS

early so that I can swing by the convenience store. There, I spend every last dollar in my wallet—a whole twenty-three bucks—on all kinds of comestibles.

Candy bars.

Cheez Doodles.

Boxes of cereal.

Packs of gum.

I stuff all the junk into my backpack, then I set out for home.

It's not too long a walk. Only about ten minutes. Seven if I speed-walk. Which, obviously, I *do*.

I spend most of that time turning a single thought over in my head:

How can a kid as brilliant as Dan Drooble be so dumb as to believe John Henry Knox's kooky ideas?

It doesn't make any sense.

Which is why, by the time I'm turning onto my street,

I'm still no closer to an answer. So I decide I'll deal with it later.

I think about Greeeg instead. About me and Greeeg. Greeeg and me. The two of us. Hanging out. Eating like crazy. Building catapults out of chopsticks.

In the future maybe lots of people will have robots for friends. Maybe I'm just ahead of my time.

And Greeeg *put himself together*. Meaning he's got construction skills, and meaning he can probably be taught other skills too. Like how to actually have a conversation. How to tease and joke and mess around.

And the farts?

The nearly lethal method of "disposal"?

It isn't really *that* bad. He must've eaten fifty pounds of food the day before, and all of that only added up to a single square turd.

That's manageable.

Right?

By the time I get inside and am on my way across the kitchen, I've got it all figured out. I just need to make a schedule, to map out exactly how much food goes into a cube and when Greeeg's most likely to dispose of it, then I can—

My thoughts are cut off by an unfamiliar sound.

It's a sort of *POCK*.

Followed by several more:

POCK-POCK-POCK.

POCK.

POCK-POCK.

POCK.

It's coming from above me. From upstairs.

I hurry out of the kitchen.

Down the hallway.

And just as I'm reaching the top of the stairs, I hear something else.

It's Greeeg.

"Dis-POSE-al COM-*pleeet*."

I don't even want to go into my bedroom. But I know I can't just stand out there in the hallway, avoiding it forever.

So I step inside and immediately see what I was afraid I would.

Only it's worse.

Instead of five or six perfectly square holes in my wall, there are about thirty. Bits of painted wood and plaster lie on the carpet beneath the damage. A cloud of white dust hangs in the air, tumbling and turning in the afternoon sun.

Greeeg's got a strip of torn duct tape hanging from his wrist, and looking at him—and at the damage he's done to my wall—*I* feel like the dumb one.

And all of a sudden another thought worms its way into my brain. I'm wondering again if Greeeg really *is* the world's greatest gift, the coolest toy imaginable, something worth bragging about to the rest of the EngiNerds. Because right then he feels a lot more like a responsibility. Like a maniac little cousin that I some-how got stuck babysitting, not a new friend. Because a friend is someone who gets you *out* of trouble, not someone who gets you *into* trouble.

Right?

29.

I KNOW IT DOESN'T MAKE ANY SENSE. AND I
know it's not fair—but looking at my busted-up wall, it's
not Greeeg or my grandpa I'm mad at, but *Dan*.

As if *he* left that box on my front porch.

As if *he* plopped this robot down in my life.

As if *he* programmed the thing to break my kitchen
window and then put a couple hundred dollars' worth
of damage in my wall.

I pace around my bedroom. I walk from the wall to
my bed. Then from my bed to my dresser. Then from
my dresser to my desk and back to my bed, so I can
start the whole thing over again.

Greeeg watches. His big metal square of a head piv-
ots on his little neck. His plastic eyes follow me, flicker-
ing and blinking randomly.

I'm muttering.

"Stupid, dumb . . . stupid idiot . . . him and John
Henry dumb-face . . . Mr. I'm So . . . what a . . . doesn't

even know . . . can't even . . . and his dumb . . . probably watching that stupid show . . . *Dumb League of Ladybug Losers* . . . stupid insects . . . stupid—"

I finally stop.

Because I've got an idea.

Not a great one.

Not even a *good* one.

It's an angry idea. One of those that you kind of know from the get-go you'll end up regretting if you actually follow through with, but that's just too tempting to ignore.

Here's what I think I'll do:

Go downstairs, turn on the TV, find the station that plays *The League of Ladybugs*, watch a few seconds—or enough so that I can get the gist of what's going on in the episode—then call up Dan and mercilessly make fun of him for spending his *Friday afternoon* sitting around ALL BY HIMSELF watching such childish nonsense.

And after shoving Greeeg back under my bed, that's what I *do* do.

Only I can't find the stupid show on TV. It's not playing on the station I thought it was on. So I flip through every channel, waiting through commercials if I have to—but *still* I can't find the thing. I even scroll through the guide. I even enter the show's name into the search bar.

It's nowhere to be found.

I stand there in the living room for a minute, just staring at the TV.

Then I go over to the computer.

I search for "the league of ladybugs" on the Internet and quickly learn the reason why I can't find any trace of the show on television.

IT GOT CANCELED.

The League of Ladybugs was taken off the air *two years ago*. And it's not like they've been showing reruns, either. Apparently, one of the show's two creators sued the other one, and they've been in some long, messy court battle ever since. It's *illegal*—as in *against the law*—for any TV station to show a single episode.

Learning this, my anger disappears. It gets zapped away, fast as lightning.

Now I'm just upset.

Hurt.

Because if Dan hasn't been watching that stupid show these past two years . . . then, well, what *has* he been doing?

30.

SATURDAY MORNING, I'M EVEN MORE EXCITED

than usual to go see my grandpa. If before I had about a billion questions to ask him about Greeeg, now I've got a billion and a half. Also, I'll admit, after a Friday afternoon and evening spent with no one but the robot . . . well, I'm feeling a little lonely. It got kind of hard to think of Greeeg as the world's coolest friend after he turned my bedroom into a disaster zone.

And, speaking of Greeeg—before I get in Dad's car, I take some extra measures to make sure he doesn't get into any trouble while I'm gone. I duct tape each of his limbs to one of the four posts of my bed, then grab my old bike lock from the basement and fasten his neck to the frame.

I don't think even Houdini could get out of this.

Then we're off to Bright Horizons. And I know I've already said that that's the name of the retirement community where my grandpa lives, but I don't think

I've explained yet just how bad of a name for the place that is.

The way it's set up—with a big central courtyard and then all these identical apartments arranged in a rectangle around it—you can't even *see* the horizon. And not even if you're on the outside of the rectangle, at one of the apartment's front doors. The whole property is surrounded by these big trees. No matter where you are at the place, there's no way you can see the horizon, not to mention figure out if it's looking bright.

But it's a nice enough place, I guess.

Grandpa seems to like it fine.

He spends his days on his little back patio, in the shade of this beach umbrella we got him one year for his birthday. He keeps a small cup full of toothpicks on the table right beside him, and he just sits there, moving one of the little wooden sticks back and forth from one side of his mouth to the other, all the while watching the goings-on in the courtyard.

On Saturday mornings that's what I do too. Dad drops me off, then heads to the grocery store to buy a week's worth of the microwavable burritos that my grandpa eats for breakfast, lunch, dinner, and any and every in-between-meal snack. While Dad's gone, I sit with Grandpa and we talk.

Well, I guess I should say that *I* talk.

Grandpa, you see, doesn't talk much.

Or at all, really.

But we get each other nonetheless. I can't explain it, and sometimes it frustrates my mom and dad—the way I can translate Grandpa's grunts and head shakes and eyebrow wiggles and shrugs into words, into questions and answers and comments and the like.

That day though, I'm more glad than ever that I can. Because if I don't get a handle on this Greeeg situation soon—well, I don't know what'll happen. But I've got a feeling it might not be too good.

31.

GRANDPA'S ALREADY OUT ON THE PATIO

when I arrive. I take a seat and ask him how he's been.

He moves the toothpick he's got in from one side of his mouth to the other. Then he shrugs his left shoulder. Then he tips his head back. Then he shrugs his *right* shoulder.

"I know," I tell him. "It's been super nice out. Just this morning Mom was saying it felt more like summer than spring."

Grandpa pulls his toothpick from his mouth and tosses it into the grass. Then he reaches over to the nearby cup and slides out a brand-new one.

I wait for him to get the toothpick settled on one side of his mouth. Then I say:

"So."

Grandpa raises the eyebrow nearest to me.

"I just—I have a few questions for you, if you don't mind."

The eyebrow lifts a little higher.

"Oh," I say. "They're about the gift."

Now Grandpa's eyebrows sink. His lips, too. They dip down around his toothpick.

He thinks for a second. Then he holds out a flat, downturned hand and moves it slowly forward.

"The train?" I say.

He nods and smiles.

"No," I tell him. "Not the train."

He's frowning again.

And me?

I'm starting to worry.

Because, what is this—a joke?

Grandpa can be funny, but this isn't his kind of humor.

"The *robot*," I say. "Greeeg."

He's still frowning at me.

"No?" I say. "Nothing? You don't have any idea what I'm talking about?"

Grandpa thinks.

He thinks *hard*.

Then he gives his head a single, decisive shake.

32.

IF GRANDPA DIDN'T GIVE ME THE ROBOT,

then who did?

I don't have a clue, and *that* gives me the creeps.

As soon as Dad stops the car in the driveway, I hop out and race inside and up to my room to make sure Greeeg's still under my bed.

I *try* to, at least. But Mom's standing there at the bottom of the stairs with her arms spread out from one banister to the other.

"Two things," she says.

I stand there and listen, but first heave a sigh to let her know that I'm kind of in a major rush.

Mom hears it, obviously, but still takes her sweet time.

Her first thing is that she and Dad are going to be gone for the rest of the day. They're going to a wedding or something, and she wants to know if I'll be all right on my own.

"Yeah," I tell her. "Sure."

The second thing Mom says is that I got a phone call while I was out—and when she says it, a big warm wave of relief sweeps over me.

"From who?" I ask her, even though I don't need to. I know who it is.

Dan, of course.

For one thing, nobody else ever calls me. And for another, *it's been almost twenty-four hours since we've talked*. That just doesn't happen. And no stupid argument about John Henry Knox and his dumb ideas should keep us from talking for *that* long. Not even the fact that Dan has been lying to me for the past two years about all that time he was supposedly spending watching *The League of Ladybugs* should do that—though, yeah, I *do* expect a decent explanation about it. But more important, *I* need to talk to *him*. To my best friend. I need to talk to him about Greeeg—*bad*.

When Mom doesn't answer me, I try again:

"Mom."

She rolls her eyes. Says:

"Why don't you check the message pad, Ken?"

That's the little pad of paper Mom keeps beside the

phone. She's been trying for years to get me and my dad into the habit of using it.

I heave a second sigh, then head to the kitchen to read the piece of paper. I reach for the phone at the same time, and even start thumbing in Dan's number.

But when my eyes actually start dragging across the words Mom wrote, I stop.

Because it's not Dan's name I'm seeing.

The pad says:

John Henry Knox.

I actually gasp.

And Mom, having now given me enough time to use her beloved message pad, steps into the kitchen behind me and says:

"He told me to tell you that he got one too. He didn't say what *one* was, just that you'd understand."

A few seconds pass.

Then a few more.

I can practically feel the color draining from my face.

"Ken?" Mom says. "*Ken.* Did you eat one of Grandpa's burritos? Are you going to be sick?"

33.

I TAKE A SECOND TO COMPOSE MYSELF. DEEP breaths. Soothing thoughts.

Then I pick up the phone and dial the digits scribbled down on the message pad.

I'm expecting John Henry Knox to answer. Or, I guess, John Henry Knox's mom or dad or one of his sisters.

What I'm not expecting is this:

"TOP of the MOR-ning. I AM *Sveeen*. Prop-or-TEE of MIS-ter John HEN-ree . . . ree . . . ree . . . ree . . . ree . . . ree . . . KNOX."

For a second, I can't do anything. Then my brain jolts into panic mode, and I've got questions—loads of them.

"Where was it? At your house? Did you see it get delivered? Was your name on the box?"

There's no answer.

Then:

"I AM *Sveeen*. Prop-or-TEE of—"

I hang up.

Wait a second.

The phone rings.

I answer.

"Hello?"

"Did you just hang up?"

It's John Henry Knox.

"Yes," I tell him. "Now are you ready to tell me what happened?"

John Henry Knox clears his throat and says, "Earlier this morning I went out to get the newspaper. The *Wall Street Journal*, if you were wondering."

"I wasn't."

"You see, I've invested in a number of start-up companies. Mostly those in the computing, robotics, and telecommunications sectors—though I do have a small amount of money in a company that builds luxury mobile disaster shelters."

"I literally couldn't care less."

"A little more than halfway down the path that leads from our veranda to the front gates, where our mailbox is located, I noticed something strange and unfamiliar clouding the periphery of my vision. I turned and

 99

saw the box. Large. Brown. Obviously repurposed. My name was on it—but there was no address. Confirming my hypothesis that the box had been hand-delivered. Now, you're surely wondering *how* I reached this hypothesis."

"Nope."

"Through observation only, by way of a series of logical inferences, I—"

I hang up here.

I've got all the information I want.

And if I have to listen to John Henry Knox for another second—well, burrito or no burrito, I really might puke.

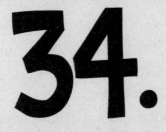

34.

THE PHONE RINGS AND RINGS, BUT I IGNORE IT.

I'm thinking.

Questioning.

Why me?

Why me and John Henry Knox?

Who, having access to these machines, would choose to give them to a couple of kids?

Maybe smarter-than-average and pretty technically proficient kids—but kids all the same.

It's almost like we, the EngiNerds, are being *targeted*.

But *why*?

The phone finally shuts up.

But a second later it's replaced by a new noise.

Knocking.

I go and answer the door.

It's Jerry, smiling his biggest smile.

I open my mouth to say hi, but before I can make a

sound, I notice what's sitting at the end of my drive-way.

A big, beaten up box.

Jerry's name is written on the side.

"It's heavy," he tells me.

Then he holds up a skateboard. Or what used to be a skateboard. Now it's in two pieces, snapped right down the middle.

Still smiling, Jerry leans toward me and whispers, "I think it's a robot."

And me?

I don't answer.

I *can't* answer.

All I can do is stand there and gape at the box while my mind spins and twirls like some sort of sickening, high-speed merry-go-round.

35.

JERRY SEEMS FINE.

But *I'm* not.

I'm confused, and worried, and even more confused still.

I don't know what to do, but what I *do* do is leave Jerry there on the porch and run inside to check on Greeeg. He's still there—thank God—taped up and locked to my bed.

Back downstairs I hurry out onto the porch and find my mom standing there talking to Jerry. She sees me panting, looking panicked, and frowns.

"Ken . . . ," she says, "is everything okay?"

I nod, because I don't trust myself to open my mouth and try to use my words.

But my mom doesn't seem convinced. She turns to Jerry.

Thankfully, he's still smiling. He gives my mom a wink, and then also a big thumbs-up.

A car horn honks.

It's my dad, in the driveway.

My mom hesitates, and I can tell she wants to ask more questions. But then my dad honks again, and instead of launching an interrogation, Mom just gives me the usual spiel—be good, be safe, call if you need anything. Then she goes.

I wait for the car to pull out of the driveway, and only then let out the breath I'd been holding in.

Then I start pacing back and forth across the porch, thinking things through.

Jerry doesn't seem to mind. He takes a seat, pulls a carton of chocolate milk from out of nowhere, and slowly sips away at it.

"So," I say.

Jerry quits his sipping long enough to say "So" too.

"This morning," I continue, "both you and John Henry Knox received packages similar to the one that I received a couple days ago. Now, I ask you, could this be a simple coincidence? Could it merely be chance that not one, not two, but *three* of us found these packages on our doorsteps?"

Jerry lets go of his straw.

"Lawn."

I turn to him.

Blink.

"What?"

Jerry smiles.

"I don't really have a doorstep. The box was on my lawn."

"Drink your milk," I tell him.

He drinks.

"The answer is no," I say, pacing again. "Not unless there were dozens, not unless there were *hundreds* of these things being distributed throughout town. And even then, the likelihood of the three of us all getting these boxes within a span of forty-eight hours? Well, even then it would be hard to believe that there wasn't something strange—something strange and *purposeful*—going on."

I turn to Jerry.

"Right?"

Jerry doesn't stop slurping his chocolate milk, but he does give me a thumbs-up.

"Right," I say. "And I don't know about you, but it doesn't seem to me like these robots are here to store food or whatever. Based on the way *mine's* behaving, I'd say they're here to *take* all our food. It's like they want us to starve or something. But what kind of a sick, twisted person would *do* that? Who would ever actually *unleash* these things? What kind of an evil lunatic would do something so irresponsible? So—so *insane*?"

This time, I'm not looking for an answer from Jerry. But he gives me one anyway. He says:

"Dan."

"Huh?"

"Dan," he says again, pointing at something over my shoulder.

I turn.

Dan's standing there at the bottom of the porch steps.

"Hey," he says. He's got his hands in his pockets, like he's embarrassed or something. "You guys have a second? I think . . . I think we should talk."

36.

I DON'T KNOW WHAT DAN WANTS TO TALK

about, but I also don't really care. Not right now.

"Dan," I say, "some kind of evil lunatic is sending EngiNerds these robots. I don't know why, but I've got a feeling that it's maybe not so good. So feel free to stick around or whatever, but right now Jerry and I are busy figuring out just who the heck is doing this to us."

Dan gulps. Then he says, "Me."

"Huh?" I say.

Dan takes a breath and then spells it out for me, nice and clear.

"Me," he says. "*I'm* the one sending EngiNerds the robots. *Me.*"

There's a sound—a hollow sort of gurgling.

It's Jerry. He's finished his carton of chocolate milk.

He sets the thing aside.

Smiles.

"That," he says, "is very, very amazing."

37.

"AMAZING?!" I SHRIEK.

Because I am *not* amazed. All I'm feeling is anger and confusion, and there's too much of them inside of me for any other emotions to fit.

But Jerry's so amazed that he's begun to giggle and clap.

"*Shut it, Jerry,*" I snap at him. Then I turn to Dan. "Another secret, huh? *More* lies? I don't know why I'm even surprised. Because I know about the show, Dan. That *stupid* TV show. It's been off the air. It's been gone for *two years*. And you've been lying to me. To *me*. For two years!"

Dan doesn't try to deny it.

"I know," he says. "And I'm sorry. I really am. But listen. Please. The robots—I think I might've . . . miscalculated." He looks straight at me. "I need your help, Ken."

"Oh really?" I say. "You do? You need *my* help?"

"I do," Dan says. "Yours and Jerry's and whoever else's."

I throw my head back and laugh.

"*My* help? *Our* help? No, no, no. Me and Jerry—which, by the way, sorry, Jerry, for snapping at you and everything—Jerry and I aren't helping *you*. That's not how it works, Dan. You don't lie to your friends for two whole years and then come and ask for their help. Nuh-uh. Get out of here. Go!"

Dan doesn't leave. Instead, he says, "I'm worried, Ken. Please. The robots—I made . . . a lot of them."

"I know," I tell him. "I've got one, and so does John Henry Knox, and now so does Jerry. That's his in the driveway."

"No," Dan says. "You don't get it. There's . . . there's—th-thuh—"

"Yes, there's *three*," I say for him. "I know how to count, Dan."

He shakes his head. And then he goes on shaking it for a good long time.

Finally, I get it.

"There's more?" I say, my voice suddenly emptied of anger and hurt. Now it's just shaky. Full of fear.

Dan nods.

 109

"O-kay," I say slowly, like the answer will be different—maybe *better*—if I ask my question carefully. "How many more than three?"

"A dozen," Dan says.

"No," I gasp.

Then, with a tiny shrug, he adds:

"Plus another three."

38.

EIGHTEEN.

One-eight.

That's how old you have to be to buy a lottery ticket, vote for president, or go and see an R-rated movie by yourself.

That's the number of eggs there are in those over-size cartons that, once you pull them out of the fridge, you can never seem to fit back in again.

That's how many kids there are in my class.

I stick with that. With the image of my classroom, every one of the desks taken up by a student.

I shut my eyes.

And I can see it.

There's Lisa.

There's Isabel.

There's Chris.

I hold them all there, in my mind . . .

And then attempt to replace each of them with a

walking, talking, bottomlessly hungry robot.

But it's not easy.

It's like my brain is trying to drag its way up a steep hill—a steep hill that keeps getting swept over with avalanches of loose gravel.

So I open my eyes back up and ask Dan the question pulsing in my brain.

"How?"

Slowly, Dan fills up his lungs with air.

Then he talks for about ten minutes straight.

He tells me and Jerry the craziest story I've ever heard. . . .

39.

BELIEVE IT OR NOT, IT ALL BEGAN WITH THAT
stupid kids' show—*The League of Ladybugs*. Well, with
the TV show and with John Henry Knox.

But first things first.

Just before *The League of Ladybugs* got canceled, in
the very last episode to ever grace the airwaves, the
band of pretty, polka-dotted insects took on its most
troublesome problem yet. They went to battle with a
gang of mechanical, motorized, and—probably most
disturbingly for the bright red, incessantly cheery
bugs—utterly emotionless beetles.

These creatures weren't kind. They weren't con-
siderate. They didn't know how to share. For them,
friendship was something strange, silly, and even
dumb.

Of course, the hyperfriendly and always-ready-to-
share-with-others ladybugs were horrified. And when
the robotic beetles began to eat all their food without

a single "please" or "thank you"? Well, that right there was the last straw. The ladybugs were going to have to—wait for it—*teach the beetles some basic manners.*

Can you believe Dan actually *liked* this stuff?

Ugh.

Anyway, that's the last part of the episode that really matters. Because the seed was planted in Dan's brain. He started thinking about robots—and got *me* to start thinking about them too. We even built a few things, like this little four-wheeled LEGO craft that could set up and knock down thirty-foot-long rows of dominoes all by itself. I thought it was all pretty nifty, but soon enough I moved on to something else. (I think, actually, that was when my grandpa sent me that build-it-your-self wind tunnel). But Dan *didn't* move on. Somehow, he decided that he could build an even bigger, better robot—and that he could do it without any of *my* help.

So he started doing research. Reading, experimenting, dreaming. He did all this during the afternoons that *The League of Ladybugs* used to air. He knew I'd have no interest in hanging out with him then, and he didn't feel so bad about lying to me, seeing as the idea for the robot was at least inspired by the now-canceled TV show— you know, the one I ragged on every chance I got.

Now, cut to a few months later, which was when John Henry Knox started telling all us EngiNerds about the bizarre, unprecedented weather patterns he'd been noticing and how it very well might mean the end of the world as we knew it. Dan, being Dan, freaked out. There was a lot of lip gnawing going on at this time.

One thing that John Henry Knox was always babbling on about was food. The need to manufacture "long-lasting comestibles" and find a way to "efficiently stockpile enormous quantities" of them.

That's when Dan had a breakthrough. Because he'd been stuck on his robot. He was in need of a nudge— or maybe even a full-on shove—in the right direction. Or in *any* direction, really. And here it was. This was it. Without even meaning to or knowing that he'd done it, John Henry Knox had given Dan a mission, a *reason* to build a robot.

It was the last thing he'd needed.

Besides, obviously, the thousands of dollars' worth of materials.

But then fate intervened. . . .

40.

ONE DAY DAN WAS WALKING THROUGH HIS

kitchen. He glanced at the messy spread of newspapers on the table as he passed by, and his eye caught on a strange sight.

It was an advertisement.

And in big, bubbly, bright orange letters, there was this:

99% OFF!!

Dan was curious.

What store would ever offer such an insane deal?

They'd be bought out of business within a couple hours.

Reading the ad more closely, Dan saw that the sale was in honor of a nearby hardware store's 99th year in business, and quickly realized that the "99%" must've been a typo. Surely it was supposed to have said "9.9%" instead. But there was no fine print. And Dan just so happened to be in need of a ridiculous—and otherwise unaffordable—amount of metal.

Dan told his dad about the misprint, and they were in the car on their way to Hardware Village within a few minutes.

The manager wasn't happy about it. But when Dan's dad threatened to take the company to court, the guy gave in, so long as these brazen customers of his didn't buy "too absurd an amount of stuff."

Dan and his dad bought an amount of stuff that was just shy of absurd. It took them six trips back and forth to get everything home.

With all the lumber he got, Dan's dad had some friends help him build a shed, plus a shelter for the brand-new grill he'd bought for just four bucks. Now he could barbecue in the rain or sleet or snow—maybe even during a potentially apocalyptic megastorm.

Dan, meanwhile, was in the basement with several hundred pounds of metal. He was building robots.

41.

AS SOON AS DAN'S DONE WITH HIS STORY, I

start asking questions.

First, I want to know how many of his eighteen robots he already distributed.

"All of them," he says, explaining that he kept some for himself and then gave one to each of the EngiNerds.

Then I start asking him about just what the robots can do—besides, that is, fart out food-cubes at speeds of nearly a hundred miles per hour.

Instead of giving me an answer, Dan says, "I think we better go see Greeeg."

I lead the way upstairs. Greeeg's under the bed, right where I left him before. Not *how* I left him though. He's somehow managed to get both arms and one leg free from the bedposts that I duct taped him to. He's also put a handful of gashes in the bike lock around his neck.

He turns his head when he notices me.

"I AM *Greeeg*," he informs me.

I sigh, stand up, and turn to Dan.

"You want me to get him out?"

Dan shakes his head frantically. Then he looks around and spots the couple dozen holes that Greeeg made in my wall yesterday afternoon. Some are square, the exact size of the food-cubes. Other holes—like in spots where a handful of the cubes all hit close together—are much larger. Dan reaches into one of the bigger holes and feels around for a minute.

"Got it," he says, pulling out one of the brown-black cubes. Then he heads out into the hallway. "Come on," he calls back to Jerry and me.

We meet him in the bathroom, where he tosses the food-cube into the bathtub. Then he motions for me and Jerry to take a few steps back from the thing. Once we've moved, he cups a hand beneath the faucet of the sink and, running the tap, gathers a tiny palmful of water.

He doesn't carry the water over to the tub. Instead, he flings it from afar, flinching back as he does so.

I'm about to ask him just what in the world he's try-ing to accomplish when there's a giant—

SQUELCH.

I turn to the bathtub.

 119

And here's what I see:

Rice cakes.

Animal crackers.

Marshmallows.

One pound of sliced turkey.

Half a cucumber.

And two grease-stained take-out containers with the General Noodles logo stamped on the front.

42.

I POINT TOWARD THE TUB.

Fortunately, Dan knows what I'm getting at. Because honestly? Just now I don't think I'm capable of stringing together a coherent sentence.

He says:

"Go ahead. It's safe."

Jerry and I go and take a closer look.

The first thing I notice about the food in the bathtub is the damage. Or I guess I should say the *lack* of damage.

Because, yeah, sure—the rice cakes got a bit beaten up. The ones at the very top and bottom of the bag have been smooshed into dust. But through the plastic packaging, I can tell that a handful of those in the center of the stack are perfectly whole.

Same with the animal crackers. A couple camels might've lost their legs. A hippo might've been beheaded. Overall, though, the little bagged zoo fared incredibly well.

The marshmallows, too, plus the turkey and the cucumber and even those take-out containers—everything looks about the same as it did when it went into Greeeg's stomach, before it got squashed down into a tiny cube.

It takes me a minute, but then I find my voice.

Well, sort of.

I say:

"This . . ."

And then I say it again:

"This . . ."

On my third try, I finally get it out:

"This is unbelievable."

Jerry agrees, giving Dan a smile, a wink, a thumbs-up, *and* holding his other hand out for a fist bump.

Then someone says, "It's beyond unbelievable. It's groundbreaking. A breakthrough component of a breakthrough machine."

I turn and look and see John Henry Knox standing there in the bathroom doorway. He's got a gash across his forehead and a gleam in his eye.

43.

"WHAT ARE YOU DOING HERE?"

John Henry Knox—who, let me take a second to remind you, just waltzed into my house, across the kitchen, down the hall, and up the stairs, and all of this without first being asked inside (which I'm pretty sure is illegal)—looks at me disgustedly. He says:

"I came here to talk to *Dan*, not you."

"Okay," I say. And just in case he somehow doesn't realize it, I add, "But you're in *my* house."

"I know," he says, giving me a look like *I'm* the crazy one.

Then he turns to Dan.

"Dan," he says, "you *are* the one building these machines, correct?"

Dan doesn't answer. He's gnawing his lip and staring at the wound on John Henry Knox's forehead.

"Wait, wait, wait," I say to John Henry Knox. "You figured that out?"

John Henry Knox smiles his smug little smile.

"Of course."

"How?"

"Well, I'm familiar with Dan's work, and Sveeen was basically plastered with his signature touches. It helped, as well, that Dan has shown an increased interest in my analyses and theories as of late, in particular the problem of food gathering and storage in potentially inhospitable environments."

John Henry Knox tips his head from side to side.

"Also," he says, "the only thing Sveeen wouldn't eat was radishes."

I turn from John Henry Knox to Dan, back and forth and back again. It's annoying. No, it's *infuriating*. I know John Henry Knox is smart, but the fact that he so easily saw Dan in his non-radish-eating robot? It's just not right. If anyone should've known that Dan was behind all this, it's me. *Me*. I mean, *I'm* the guy's best friend.

"Okay," I tell John Henry Knox. "All right. You came. You talked to Dan. Now, if you don't mind, we're pretty busy."

"I know," he says.

And I sigh.

"Do you know *everything*?" I ask him.

"Nope," he says. "But I do know quite a lot. And I know that it would be wise for us to sit down and exchange some information."

Jerry says, "Like about why your forehead's bleeding?"

"Yeah," I say. "And about how you got into my house."

John Henry Knox answers Jerry's question first.

"That's why I came here," he says.

He points up at his forehead.

"Sveeen—he was trying to get away. To get down the street. And when I tried to stop him . . . he resorted to violence."

When I hear this, my insides form a giant knot. I look over at Dan, hoping he'll shake his head and say that no, that's impossible, one of *his* robots would never do such a thing.

Instead, he lifts up his T-shirt. And there, on his stomach, are a handful of purple-black bruises. Each of them is the size of a bunched-up robot claw.

The four of us are silent for several seconds.

Then John Henry Knox answers the question that I asked him, the one about how he got into my house.

"Also," he says, "your front door was wide open."

44.

I BARREL BY DAN AND JERRY AND JOHN

Henry Knox and head for the stairs. But before I'm even halfway down them, I find solid evidence that what I'm worried about has, indeed, happened.

Kitty has taken himself out for a stroll around the neighborhood.

The lamp that usually sits on the little table beside the couch is gone, and the extension cord into which it has been plugged for the past decade has been dragged halfway across the room. Across the room—and toward the front door.

"Oh wow," I say, heading that way. "Okay."

I close the door behind me and immediately start calling out for Kitty.

But that turns out to be unnecessary. I find the pooch pretty much immediately.

He's sitting at the bottom of the porch steps, whining a tiny high-pitched whine and staring down at the pieces of the shattered lamp littering our walkway. He looks up when he notices me. Gives a little yip. Like he's asking me to take over and fix this situation—*stat*.

"Kitty."

I go down to comfort him.

"This is what happens," I tell him, "when you mix gravity and ceramic and cement."

Kitty yips again.

"I know, I know," I say, tugging gently on his left ear—which sounds strange, I know, but is the dog's favorite way to be "petted."

I start to clean up Kitty's mess for him, but only a couple seconds in, I sense someone else standing there. Or *several* someone elses.

When I look up, the guys are all there, ranged side by side at the top of the steps. They look about as upset as Kitty.

Dan's the one who breaks the news.

"Your back door's open too," he says.

And I know what's coming next. I just do.

But Dan says it anyway:

"Greeeg's gone."

45.

I'M READY TO DASH INTO THE STREET AND chase the robot down. But none of the other guys seem to think that this is such a great idea.

Actually, it's mostly John Henry Knox who gives me this impression.

"Please, Kennedy," he says. "Now's not the time to be stupid or rash—and certainly not *both*."

Then he once again suggests that we sit down and exchange some information. This time, he says it's "imperative" that we do so.

"Really?!" I ask him. "You really want to *sit down* while there's a bunch of these robots out there, on the loose?"

"Yes," he answers. "I do. We're only going to make matters worse if we go out there without any semblance of a plan."

Dan gives me a look like he agrees with John Henry Knox.

Jerry seems to too.

So we go inside and sit ourselves down around the kitchen table.

Dan, being the one with all the information, starts the exchange.

"The robots are primarily programmed to obtain and store comestibles," he says. "In order to do that, their brains, so to speak, are full of recognizable pictures of human food. Fruits. Veggies. Bags of bread. Boxes of crackers. Everything. However, they also possess a rudimentary form of intelligence."

"Meaning?" I ask.

"Meaning," says Dan, "that they learn. They develop a sort of memory bank. The longer they're active, the larger this bank becomes."

"So they can begin to converse," says John Henry Knox.

Dan bobs his head back and forth.

"Sort of," he says. "They can say 'hi.' Tell you their name. Tell you *your* name. After a certain amount of time they could, probably, give you walking directions to somewhere close by or tell you how to perform some simple task."

Dan pauses.

 129

"Also . . . ," he says, "they learn how to—well, how to *overcome* any obstacles that might be preventing them from obtaining food."

He sounds kind of scared saying this.

I don't get why.

John Henry Knox, though, seems to have an idea. He looks extremely excited. He says:

"So they can gather in zones potentially inhospitable to human life!"

"Um," I say. *"What?"*

"Say for some reason humans can't go outside," Dan tells me. "Say they've got to stay indoors, or even underground, in a basement or a bunker, because there are megatwisters or super hurricanes raging up above. The robots could be sent out and counted on to collect anything edible in a certain area. They could not only survive the storms, but, say, pick through the rubble of a fallen building to get at the refrigerator full of food inside."

"Okay," I say. "Obstacles."

I'm nodding now, finally grasping things, seeing how all these pieces fit together.

"And then," I say, "when the bots get back, all you need is a few drops of water and—*boom*. A bunker full of snacks. That's brilliant."

Dan nods.

And I wait for him to say more.

But he doesn't.

And it leaves me with the distinct feeling that I'm *still* missing something.

Jerry looks a bit confused too. Even John Henry Knox has his thinking face on.

"So," I finally say. "Greeeg and Sveeen and all the others—they're gonna gobble up everything they can find, then come back to our 'bunkers' to give it to us, right? Kind of like they're our own personal butlers or something. And then, once they're back, all we've got to do is . . ."

I don't finish. It's because of the look on Dan's face. He looks straight-up terrified, and he's staring at the gash on John Henry Knox's forehead again.

"What?" I say. "What is it?"

"I don't think it'll be that easy," Dan says. "I think . . . I think maybe the robots are learning to see *us* as obstacles. Human beings."

Oh.

So *that's* the part I was missing.

Oh no.

46.

DAN HAS SOME PHONE CALLS TO MAKE.

Before we do a thing, he says, we need to get a handle on where all the robots are and what kind of state they're in. His plan is to call each one of the EngiNerds.

We leave him to it, and Jerry and John Henry Knox and I head into the living room to give him some space. I turn on the TV, but not because I actually want to watch it. I'm just trying to keep us distracted while we wait. The *Channel 5 News* is on, and I turn it way down so we can listen in on Dan.

Every one of his phone conversations is more or less the same. First he asks each of the EngiNerds if he got the package yet, and then if he built the thing inside of it—or if the thing inside of it built *itself*—and, if so, what happened next.

Of course, there's always a little interlude when the guy on the other end of the line finds out it was Dan who designed, manufactured, and programmed the walking, talking, food-obsessed robots.

Dan's side, though, goes like this:

"Hey, Simon," he says.

Or "Rob" or "Amir" or "Alan" or "Chris."

Then:

"Nothing much, what about you . . . ?"

"Oh really . . . ?"

"Did you open it . . . ?"

"Yeah, and then it put itself together . . ."

"No. I'm actually the one who . . ."

"Yep. Ha. Seriously serious . . ."

"Uh-huh . . ."

"Yep, yeah . . ."

"Ha. Well, thanks . . ."

"Anyway . . ."

"Oh, it did . . . ?"

"I'm sorry to hear that . . ."

"Wow. That's different. . . ."

"Oh God . . ."

"Okay. Thanks, Simon."

Or "Rob" or "Amir" or "Alan" or "Chris."

Once he's done, Dan comes slouching into the

living room. I can tell by his posture alone that the news he's got to deliver isn't good.

"Almost everyone's bot is up and running," he says, eyes aimed down at the carpet. "And eating," he adds. "And . . ." He pauses to blow the air out of his cheeks. "Attacking."

Still staring down at the carpet, he gives us some of the details.

"Apparently Chris's did the same thing as mine— sucker punched him in the gut and ran out the door."

"Oof," Jerry says.

"Max's stomped on his foot. He's pretty sure the thing broke a couple of his toes."

"Yikes," says Jerry.

"Alan got headbutted."

"Ouch."

Jerry again, obviously.

Dan stops there. He goes on staring down at the carpet. Slowly, desperately, he shakes his head.

And despite everything—the secrets, the lies—I feel bad for the guy. After all, he's still my best friend. And, I mean, he did something incredible. And since then— yeah, sure, things have kind of spun out of control. But *he did something incredible.* He'd gone and one-upped us all. From now on, any project an individual EngiNerd tackled would pale in comparison to Dan's.

I know it's not exactly the time to celebrate the guy's achievements, but I hate to see him like this. And so, in an attempt to cheer him up, to stay as positive about the situation as possible, to find the silver lining in this big black cloud, I say:

"You said *almost* everyone's."

"Yeah," Dan says. "Edsley. He hasn't even opened the box."

"And you told him not to?" says John Henry Knox.

"Of course," Dan says.

"And Jerry's, too," I say. "His is still boxed up out front."

"So, sixteen," says John Henry Knox. "Sixteen robots."

"Sixteen hungry, violent robots," says Dan.

The four of us are silent for a minute. And then I give voice to the question that's already there, crowding the living room along with us.

"So what do we do?"

47.

WE DISCUSS OUR OPTIONS.

Should we call the cops?

If we did, would they even believe us?

And if they *did* believe us, what could they really do?

Would a small-town police force be able to deal with sixteen of these robots?

Also, how much trouble would we—or just Dan—get into once the cops knew that we had something—or, okay: *everything*—to do with all this?

We decide to table the idea of calling the cops for a second.

Then John Henry Knox fires a whole bunch of technical questions at Dan.

Do the robots have an emergency kill switch?

Answer: "No."

Would it be possible to wirelessly interfere with their programming?

Answer: "Doubtful."

Did Dan pretreat the metal he used so that it would be less reactive to magnetization?

Answer: "Of course."

John Henry Knox heaves a sigh.

Then, a beat later, his eyes go wide and his mouth drops open. I'm assuming it's because he just came up with some kind of amazing, foolproof idea to fix all our problems, and I feel a sudden surge of gratitude for the kid and his big, annoying, brilliant brain.

But John Henry Knox doesn't say a word. He just sits there, stunned, staring at the—

The TV.

It's still tuned to the *Channel 5 News*, and I look over just in time to see a thick black bar clank across the middle of the screen. A second later, steel gray letters pound onto the bar. And just before a shower of bright orange sparks obscures them, I see that the letters spell out two words:

ROBOTS ATTACK.

48.

I GRAB THE REMOTE AND TURN THE VOLUME

way up. A second after I do, the camera cuts to a shot of the *Channel 5 News* team's studio and then swoops in on the team's lead anchor, a lady named Cindy. She looks about as serious as I've ever seen her, and I'm so scared to hear what she has to say, I nearly change the channel.

"Yes, ladies and gentlemen—ro-*bots*. Plural. If you've been following Channel 5's continuing coverage of today's bizarre events, you already know about the incident at the farmers' market, where witnesses claim a robotic assailant absconded with several hundred dollars' worth of local produce. Now we're getting reports of a second incident, this one outside of the Flour Power Bakery. According to witnesses, there were *multiple* robotic assailants involved in this incident. The *Channel 5 News* team is advising local residents to stay inside, lock your doors, and—most of all—keep your television tuned to Channel 5 for our ongoing coverage of this story.

"And now," Cindy says, straightening a stack of papers on her desk, "back to John Castle in the field."

The camera cuts to a shot of a bakery. I know the place. It's maybe half a mile away from the parking lot where the farmers' market is held every weekend.

There's a scuffling sound offscreen and then John Castle stumbles into the shot. He's pale, as colorless as a marshmallow, and he keeps peering up and down the street, spinning suddenly to see who—or *what*—might be behind him.

After a second, a lady appears. She plucks the microphone out of John Castle's hand, then brings it up way too close to her mouth.

"Name's Rhonda," she says. "And I seen 'um. Two of 'um. Maybe three, now that I'm thinkin' about it. Big guys though. All gray. Hungry. *Angry*. Claws like—"

She lifts her free hand and twists the fingers this way and that.

"—like—kinda like that. And then they were doing this thing too. This thing—"

Rhonda suddenly drops into a crouch and pokes her butt way out behind her. And then, into the microphone, she makes a bunch of laserlike sound effects.

Pew.

Pew.

Pew-pew-pew-pew-BLAM!

The noises frighten John Castle, who takes off running down the street.

A beat later we're back in the studio with Cindy. Her face is grave, her voice severe.

"Yes, folks," she says. "You heard it here on Channel 5 first. *It seems as though these robots are capable of shooting lasers out of their rear ends.*"

49.

DAN LEAPS UP FROM THE COUCH AND RUSHES

into the kitchen. Honestly, I wouldn't have been too surprised if he didn't stop running until he reached the West
Coast, or at least made it to Texas. But he comes back
just a couple seconds later with a sheet of blank paper
and a mechanical pencil in his hand.

He plops himself down in front of the coffee table
and thumbs the eraser of the pencil to get a bit of
lead. Then he starts to sketch. First, he makes a series
of close-together parallel lines, and below and above
them a bunch of rectangles and squares.

I realize what it is just as the others do.

"Streets and buildings," says John Henry Knox, right
as Jerry says, "A map."

Dan keeps drawing.

All the way over on the left side of the paper he
makes a large square, and right in the center of it
he writes *FM*. Then, in a small rectangle toward the

paper's middle, he writes *B*. And finally, in a shape so big only a fraction of it fits on the right side of the paper, he writes *S&S*, and then draws a familiar little logo—a cartoon apple and a smiling orange slice.

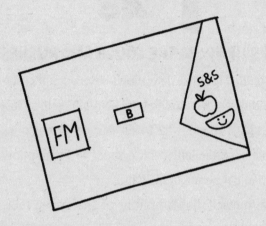

It's only then that I get just what Dan's map is of. The part of town that the robots—or at least some of them—are in. And the reason *why* they're there is obvious. You can see it as soon as you look at the paper. But just in case the day's events have totally fried my or Jerry's or John Henry Knox's brain, Dan draws an arrow. It's perfectly straight, and it runs directly from the farmers' market, past the bakery, to the Shop & Save.

"They can see the fruit," Dan says, dragging the tip

of the pencil around and around the grocery store's logo, circling the thing until the happy little fruits are trapped in the center of a giant target. "They recognize it. It looks like a picture in their memory banks, and they're heading right for it."

Looking down at Dan's map, I realize it's all over. I don't know what the other guys are thinking, but I know there's nothing we can possibly do.

We have to call the cops. Call them and tell them everything we know and do our best to make sure they actually believe us, because only then will they call up the army and the air force, who I'm thinking they just might need in order to put a stop to things.

Slowly, Dan and Jerry and John Henry Knox and I all look up from the map.

"Guys," I tell them. "I think—"

That's as far as I get. Because that's when it hits me. And it hits me like a freight train. Like a freight train barreling downhill *and* being pulled by a squadron of sound barrier–breaking, sonic boom–making, air force–grade jet planes.

I'm thinking about that food-cube Dan put in my bathtub, and how it basically *exploded* when he threw a little water on it. I'm thinking about that and about a dozen other things—like last summer, and Dan's brother, and General Noodles, just to name a few.

And then I'm pointing to Dan's map, to the parallel lines that run alongside the Shop & Save. I can see the place in my head. It's a narrow alleyway, lined with Dumpsters and piles of broken-down cardboard boxes.

"This is the *back* of the store, right?" I ask.

Dan nods.

"And all these streets over here," I say, waving my fingertip around the lines between the bakery and the grocery store. "They're all residential, yeah?"

"Yep," Jerry says. He points to a spot on the map. "My cousin lives right there."

"And so," I go on, "if people do what they've been told and stay in their houses, the robots—they shouldn't meet anybody else on their way to the Shop & Save. And before they get *into* the Shop & Save, they have to make it all the way down the alleyway."

"Right, right—all of it's right," says John Henry Knox, trying to hurry me along. "What are you getting at?"

I look at John Henry Knox and Jerry, and ask them a single, simple question.

"Have you guys ever worked with chopsticks?"

Beside them, Dan's face lights up.

So does mine.

50.

FIRST THING I DO IS RUN UP TO MY CLOSET
and dig out all the pairs of chopsticks I've gathered
from years and years of ordering from General Noodles.
There's no time to count, but if I had to guess, I'd say
I've got hundreds, if not a thousand, of the thin little
strips of wood.

I stuff as many of them as I can into an old backpack, then grab two of the shoe boxes that live on my
bookshelf. One of them is labeled RUBBER BANDS, the
other one is labeled BALLOONS.

Back downstairs, before I even get a chance to put
the backpack down, Dan grabs a handful of the chopsticks out of it. Then he takes a seat and shows Jerry
and John Henry Knox step-by-step how to build a catapult, using the same design we put to work last summer
on Dan's older brother. Within sixty seconds both guys
get it—they're EngiNerds, after all—and wave Dan off
so they can start constructing their own.

I'm hesitant to interrupt, but I do so just to let them know that if they've got the catapults covered, I'm going to fill up the balloons and gather as many jugs and bottles of water as I can find.

A second later I'm darting toward the kitchen. Before I can get *into* the kitchen though, Dan calls out to me.

"Wait!"

I spin around in time to see the smile spread across his face.

"This is gonna work," he tells me.

I stand there long enough to flash him a smile back, and then I'm on my way again. But my smile doesn't last. It's gone before I even get to the sink. Because I'm not feeling quite as confident as Dan seems to be.

Filling up one balloon after another, I hope as hard as I can hope that this crazy plan I just cooked up really does work.

51.

NINETEEN MINUTES.

That's how long it takes.

Nineteen minutes for me to make a ton of water balloons and gather up as many jugs and bottles of water as I can find.

Nineteen minutes for Dan and Jerry and John Henry Knox to construct enough catapults for us to launch a serious attack on a horde of hungry robots.

Nineteen minutes—and then another one or two for us to carefully pack it all up and get out the door.

And then we're off. We're on our way to Shop & Save, moving as fast as four not-so-athletic kids carrying a couple dozen gallons of water and a handful of super fragile, chopstick-and-rubber-band catapults can.

LUCKILY, WE DON'T RUN INTO ANY ROBOTS

on the way to the grocery store. That, of course, could be for any number of reasons—some good, some bad, and others downright ugly.

I point Dan and John Henry Knox toward the alley-way in back of the store.

"Go set up," I tell them. "I'll be right there."

Then I grab Jerry and give him some directions. First, I tell him, he needs to do a full sweep of the store. Once he's sure there are no robots inside, he's to come back out and do a loop of the place's perimeter. He's the fastest one of the four of us—a fact he made plain on the journey down to the store.

"Meet us out back as soon as you're done," I tell him, giving his shoulder a slap of encouragement.

Jerry gives me a thumbs-up and hurries off.

I book it to the back of the store, where Dan and John Henry Knox have already set up and positioned several catapults. I get out the one I'm carrying and set it up too. Then we form an assembly line and quickly pile up forty water balloons—a little more than half of the total number we've got.

"What now?" Dan says.

"Now?" I say to him and John Henry Knox. "Now we wait. . . ."

53.

AND SO WE WAIT.

But not for long.

Two, maybe three minutes later, we see a bright spot of light just past the narrow gap in the cement barriers that separate the nearby dead-end street from the alleyway. The spot of light is spiked and twinkling, like a star that fell from the sky and touched down right here, in back of a grocery store.

Which, obviously, couldn't happen. It's a robot, its body made of highly reflective metal.

But it *looks* like a star.

And the longer I stand there waiting, the more it *feels* like it too. Like the sun itself came down from its perch up in the center of our solar system and set up shop just a hundred feet from me for the sole purpose of sucking all the moisture out of my body.

I'm sweating.

Standing in the alleyway behind the Shop & Save with a fat red water balloon in my hand, a chopstick catapult locked back and ready to be loaded at my feet, and the safety of the whole town depending on whether I and three other twelve-year-olds can pull this off, I'm sweating like I've never sweat in my life.

The robot slips through the gap and into the alley . . .

And my heart does a crazy little dance.

The robot steps into the shadow cast by the back of the grocery store, its twinkling brilliance disappearing all at once . . .

And my lungs lose their rhythm.

The robot may or may not know we're here. I can't tell for sure. It's got its big square head tipped all the way back, its plastic eyes aimed up at the giant SHOP & SAVE sign perched over our heads.

Seventy feet.

Sixty-five.

Now sixty.

The water balloon John Henry Knox has in his hand suddenly bursts.

I look over long enough to see that the guy's in even worse shape than I am. He's not only gushing sweat by the gallon, but he's shaking, too, shivering like he's got some kind of fever.

Forty feet.

Out of the corner of my eye I see Dan hand John Henry Knox a new water balloon.

Thirty-five feet.

Now thirty.

In a second, as long as it doesn't stop or change directions, the robot will be in range of our catapults.

Twenty-five feet.

Dan gets down on one knee. He holds a green water balloon right above the hand of a catapult's long, strong, ready-to-snap arm. From here, it'll take him no more than half a second to place the balloon, take aim, and launch the thing at the robot.

Twenty feet.

Eighteen.

"Make the call," Dan tells me. "Just say when."

Sixteen feet.

Fourteen.

Twelve.

"Ken."

It's Dan again. Sounding slightly worried. Because

he probably should've launched the balloon by now.

Ten feet.

Okay—he *definitely* should've launched the balloon by now.

But I can't give the command. I just noticed something. The robot—it's got a strand of duct tape dangling from each of its wrists and trailing from both ankles. There's half a bike lock hanging down over its chest like some kind of weird necklace.

Eight feet.

"Greeeg?"

The robot stops. His big square head swivels on his tiny neck. He looks down from the SHOP & SAVE sign. He looks down at me.

His eyes flash red.

He says:

"Good MOR-ning sun-SHINE."

54.

GREEEG STAYS WHERE HE IS, EIGHT FEET

away.

I take a step forward and make it seven feet.

Then another.

Six.

Behind me, Dan says:

"Ken?"

And then, when I don't answer him:

"Ken."

But Greeeg starts up before I can answer Dan.

"Sun-SHINE," the robot says. "Please FEED please. Com-EST-ib-ulls please."

"Get away from him," Dan tells me. "Get away from him *now*. You're an obstacle to him, Ken. That's it. That's all."

"I AM *Greeeg*," says Greeeg, as if defending himself against Dan's claims. "Please FEED *Greeeg* sun-SHINE."

"Run, Ken. Run now."

"Sun-SHINE. Re-MEM-ber good TIMES had at lo-CAY-shun two-NINE-three-NINE-two-two-two-two-two-two-NINE."

"Don't listen to him, Ken."

"FEED-ing . . ."

"Back away."

"Di-GES-ting . . ."

"Come on, Ken."

"Dis-POSE-al . . ."

"Please," Dan says.

And then there's silence.

Greeeg's said his piece.

Dan's said his.

Now it's up to me.

"Here," I say, holding out my hand.

Greeeg reaches for the water balloon.

I tug it back just before one of his finger-claws pops the thing.

"No," I say. "Open up."

And the universe holds its breath . . .

But nothing happens.

Until it does.

With a creak, the little door in Greeeg's torso swings open.

I peer into the robot's stomach and look for a safe place to set the water balloon. Because it's crowded in there—Greeeg's been eating. I see a paper cup from Burger Zone, a few used napkins, several rock-hard wads of already chewed gum, and three rotting oranges. I don't see any of those brown-black cubes, but I know there's got to be a few of them in there somewhere—and all I can do is hope that a nice big drink of water will make those bad boys burst.

I set the balloon atop the Burger Zone cup. It fits snugly, but not *too* snugly.

I pull my hand back. Say:

"See how that tastes."

Greeeg shuts the door to his guts and then presses the tiny button beside it.

There's a loud sound.

It's a churning and a crunching.

Behind me, Dan says:

"Okay. Now you really need to run."

55.

DAN AND JOHN HENRY KNOX ARE ALREADY

on the move by the time I turn around and start running. I don't make it too far before it happens—"it" being the explosion—but far enough so that the blast leaves me relatively unharmed.

"Blast," though, isn't really the right word.

It's more of a *SQUAH-POOM*—a massive squelch, cut off prematurely by a *pop-boom* sort of thing.

But no matter what you call it, one thing's for sure—it's powerful. It knocks me off my feet. It feels like a giant hand just scoops me up and flings me down the alleyway.

I hit the ground and slide a few feet across the pavement, shredding up my elbows and knees. But I manage to get my hands over my head just in time to keep any flying parts—nuts and bolts and hunks of busted-apart metal and, less threateningly, rice cakes and deli meat and a bunch of overripe bananas—from cracking my skull.

Once I'm sure the robot pieces are done falling out of the sky, I uncover my head and look around.

Dan's already on his feet.

John Henry Knox is halfway there.

Dan comes over and offers me a hand. He pulls me up and then looks me over, making sure I'm all right.

Which I am. A bit banged and bloodied up, but all things considered, I'm okay. Dan is too. And while John Henry Knox might've taken a couple bolts to the back, he looks fine. Maybe even a little bit excited.

That's when he giggles—a sound I never even knew the kid was capable of making.

"I wanna try," he says.

"Well," Dan tells him, jerking his chin toward the end of the alleyway, "I'm pretty sure you're gonna get a chance."

I look, and through the haze of smoke hanging over the heap of metal that had once been Greeeg, I see three more robots slipping through the cement barriers and into the alleyway.

56.

WE DART BACK TO THE CATAPULTS AND
quickly check to make sure they're still okay. One of
them is definitely unusable—it got crushed by a big
hunk of robot head and a container of cold ravioli—but
the others are fine.

I go to grab us some water balloons. But instead of
finding a pile of the things, I find a mess of stringy wet
plastic.

Obviously, I realize.

The fragile balloons were no match for the storm of
shrapnel that blew through the alleyway.

"Catch."

I look up, and Dan lobs a brand-new water balloon
my way. By the time I catch the thing, he's already
begun to prepare another.

"Ready."

That would be John Henry Knox. He's down, knees
on the pavement, right beside me. He's using one hand

to press down the arm of a catapult. The other one he's holding up to me.

I set the water balloon in his palm.

He gets it loaded.

"Say the word," he tells me.

I check on the robots. The one in front has made it just a few feet into the alleyway. The other two seem to have gotten jammed up at the entrance.

"Wait for it . . . ," I say.

The robot already in the alleyway tips its head back to take in the SHOP & SAVE sign. With its flashing eyes fastened to the thing, it picks up speed. It starts moving way faster than I ever saw Greeeg go.

"Whoa, whoa, whoa," I say. And then, hoping that I'm judging this right:

"FIRE!"

John Henry Knox releases the catapult and sends the balloon rocketing through the air. It sails beautifully—and then sails beautifully some more. It goes right over the approaching robot's head, landing much closer to the other two robots, who are still stuck at the barriers.

But Dan's on it. He's already crouched down over a catapult, loading and aiming a fat blue balloon. He lets

 161

it fly—and sends the balloon splattering directly into the approaching robot's chest.

Only this doesn't stop the thing.

There's no *SQUAH-POOM*.

The soaking wet robot keeps rushing our way.

"Um, what?" I say.

"Just wait," John Henry Knox tells me. "It'll take a little longer. But the water will get there. It should—"

There's a zap.

A single loud *PZZZZT*.

The robot charging our way suddenly changes direction. It takes a sharp right turn and smashes full speed into the side of the Shop & Save. Its bulky square head pops off its tiny neck as if it's on a spring. The rest of the robot crumples into a heap against the wall. The debris gives a few more smaller zaps. And then—the grand finale—a series of *SQUAH-POOM*s. They're nowhere near as epic as Greeeg's, but it still makes for a pretty satisfying sight.

Dan, though, doesn't even bother watching. Instead, he fetches a few more balloons. He hands one to me and one to John Henry Knox and hangs on to one for himself.

"Shall we?" he says, eyes aimed toward the narrow

entrance of the alleyway, where those other two robots have somehow managed to get their limbs tangled together.

We all take a knee, load our catapults, and fire.

John Henry Knox nails one of the robots in the shoulder.

Dan gets the other one in the back.

A second later, mine smacks right into the robots' knotted legs.

The zapping begins instantly.

And shortly after—the *SQUAH-POOM*s.

But there's no time to relax.

Not far behind the new pile of busted-apart robots, there's another pair.

And behind them, just now coming into sight—a pack of four more.

THE NEXT FEW MINUTES ARE A TOTAL BLUR.

Here's what you need to know:

Those two robots in front—they get distracted by a Dumpster that got overturned in one of the explosions and hunker down beside it to fill up on a few dozen pounds' worth of spoiled groceries.

And the pack of four bots in back—they ignore the mess and leap over the cement barriers and into the alleyway.

Yes, you read that right.

The robots *leap* over the barriers.

When I see it, my jaw drops. Literally. And my brain? It does a couple somersaults, trying—and failing—to account for what I just saw.

Dan helps me out:

"They're learning," he says. "They saw those other two get stuck, and now they know it's dangerous."

I don't immediately grasp the significance of this.

But it becomes pretty clear once we start launching some of the last of our water balloons—*and the robots dodge them*.

They step out of the way or use their strong, flexible legs to contort into crazy shapes until the balloons fly by. And when Dan fires an un-dodge-able balloon at the robot leading the charge toward us, the thing just sticks out a claw so that the balloon pops, harmlessly, several feet in front of it.

"Um, guys?" I say.

The robots continue coming toward us—the four barrier-leapers in front, and then the other two, evidently done scooping clean that nasty Dumpster, in back.

"I know this was my plan and everything. But, well, I'm kind of out of ideas here."

"AAAAAAAAARRRGGHH!!!"

The roar sends me jumping about four feet up into the air. When I touch down again, I see John Henry Knox charging the robots with an open jug of water in each hand. He gets right in the middle of the pack and does a kind of wild dance, flinging his arms around, spinning in circles, screaming like a maniac.

Dan and I watch him splash two robots good

enough to get them *PZZZZT*ing, then we grab what's left of the water and join the battle.

The first robot I go up against tries to headbutt me, but I step aside and dump a bottle of water right on the back of its head.

I yell for the guys to take cover and then run away myself. I get far enough so that the bolts that hit my back feel like mosquito bites and the Italian sub that slaps across my face feels like—well, that actually still feels like an Italian sub.

Dan gets one next.

"HIT THE DECK!" he calls out.

I duck and cover my head and a second later see a box of Flavor Shapes cereal go cartwheeling by.

Back in the thick of things, John Henry Knox and I team up on a robot who couldn't resist eating the comestibles piling up at its feet.

We turn to Dan just in time to see him hurl a bottle at the last of the six robots—and hurl it hard enough so that the plastic snaps and the water soaks the thing.

And then it's the usual:

PZZZZT.

SQUAH-POOM!

A bunch of grapes, a rotisserie chicken, and what

 166

appears to be a potted plant fly up into the air, do a few flips, and then come crashing back down to earth.

We all watch, then stand there panting, sweating, catching our breath.

Finally, John Henry Knox says:

"So there was that first one."

"Greeeg," I say.

"Plus three more," says Dan.

"Making four," I say.

"After which came those two by the Dumpster," says John Henry Knox.

"Then that big group," says Dan. "How many were in there?"

"Four," I say. "I counted. There were definitely four."

"So four plus two plus four," says Dan.

"Ten," says John Henry Knox. "Meaning there's how many left?"

"Not counting Jerry's and Edsley's, remember," I say.

"Right," says Dan. "So six."

"Where could they be?" asks John Henry Knox. "Also," he adds a second later, "where *is* Jerry?"

58.

JERRY.

He's been gone a long time.

Maybe *too* long a time.

I'm about to take off toward the front of the Shop & Save to look for him when Dan holds up a hand.

"You hear that?" he says.

It's a series of slapping sounds. Like sneakers hitting pavement.

The sounds get louder and louder—and then Jerry comes tearing around the corner. He's running fast, straight for us, his eyes wide and terrified.

Right behind him are the robots. All six of them.

And we've got only half a bottle of water left.

59.

THE ONLY THING I CAN THINK TO DO IS RUN
around to the front of the store, head inside, and grab a
few more jugs of water before the robots reach us.

Which is a long shot, I know. And probably useless,
anyway. We could get to the front of the store faster
than the robots, but not *that* much faster. By the time we
got our hands on some water, they'd probably already
be eating—and sucker punching and foot stomping
and headbutting—their way down Aisle 3.

What we need is a miracle.

And—preposterously—we get one.

First the sun disappears. The light glinting off the
smooth silver gray bodies of the robots just all of a
sudden vanishes.

I look up, confused, and see a massive, sky-span-
ning cloud racing toward us. It's like a shopping mall
or a football stadium flying through the sky, except the
cloud isn't really shaped like either of those things. It's

shaped like—well, kind of like a UFO. Like a UFO that's camouflaged as a giant white cloud, shooting down a big laser beam that's camouflaged as even *more* clouds.

"*That*," John Henry Knox shrieks, "is the most fantastic cumulonimbus I have ever seen! Look at that anvil dome! My God! What I wouldn't give to be up there at the tropopause, looking down on this beauty! That peak must be twenty thousand meters!"

It's right then that the wind picks up. Within a couple seconds, it's roaring with a deafening intensity down the alleyway. It blasts into our faces, peels back our lips, and reaches its cold, rushing hands down our throats.

But the robots are faring even worse.

One gets blown sideways and, in a desperate attempt to keep its balance, grabs on to a second, which sends them both toppling to the ground.

Seeing this, the other robots stop. They spread their legs, plant their feet, and hold their long, flexible arms out to their sides.

But then comes the rain.

Yes: *rain*.

Water.

Gobs of it.

Just pouring out of the sky.

 170

The robots get pelted. There's nowhere to run for cover—and that's if they even knew to do so. Two seconds in and they're soaked beyond hope.

And two seconds after *that* the zapping begins.

Followed by the *SQUAH-POOM*s.

And what do Dan and John Henry Knox and I do?

We laugh.

We dance.

Pummeled by the wind and rain and every kind of comestible imaginable, we celebrate.

Then we get Jerry out of the Dumpster he jumped into and let him know that everything's fine.

60.

THE STORM STOPS AS ABRUPTLY AS IT BEGAN.

That giant, laser-beaming UFO of a cloud drifts over us and disappears. Then the sun comes out—and with a vengeance. It's like the big, burning star is angry that the cloud covered it up. So it hammers down on us, slurping up the wetness off the pavement like the last sip of a soda through a straw. You can practically *hear* it.

We start heading back to my house, and I can't help but say it:

"That was so . . . weird."

John Henry Knox grins.

"Remember that hailstorm?" he says.

I nod, thinking back to that night—not so long ago, though it feels like forever—that Greeeg shot a food-cube through the kitchen window, waking up my parents and almost getting me grounded for the rest of my earthly existence.

"That night," says John Henry Knox, "I spotted an

almost identical cloud formation. I was able to get a few photographs and downloaded some others from the National Weather Service. However, not having been directly beneath the hail cloud, there's no way for me to be sure if it was as large as the one from today."

It sounds crazy—no, no, no, it *is* crazy—but I find myself curious about clouds—*clouds*—in a way that I never could've imagined I'd be before, and, also—this right here being the craziest part of all—I find myself kind of wanting to hear a little more about John Henry Knox's nutty, weather-related ideas.

But it's been a long day.

So I just say:

"Hm."

Back at my house we find the box containing Jerry's robot how we left it. Pretty much, at least. It got soaked, and then quick-dried by the sun, leaving the cardboard sunken in here and there.

We haul the thing inside and unpack the nuts and bolts and the slabs and sheets of metal. Then we grab some smaller boxes and bags from the basement and distribute the pieces and parts among them. Finally, Dan divides the heap of packages into four smaller piles.

"We'll each take one," he tells us.

The rest of us nod, seeing and agreeing with the wisdom of this. It's like breaking up a secret code and giving a little piece of it to a bunch of different people. It keeps any one person from making a mistake, from following through with a potentially disastrous idea.

Once we're done, we all just stand there, too tired to do much more than breathe and blink.

Except for Jerry.

"Chocolate milk?" he says.

And before any of us can say a thing, he pulls four little cartons of the stuff from out of nowhere.

61.

WE DRINK OUR CHOCOLATE MILK AND EAT

some pizza—John Henry Knox bought us a couple pies—and then just lie around in the living room, doing a whole bunch of nothing. We've got the TV on. It's tuned to Channel 5, and the news team is doing this whole big thing about the cops who found all the busted-up robot parts behind the Shop & Save. The cops, not us, are getting all the credit for saving the day. But honestly, I don't mind.

I don't think I've ever been so exhausted in my life. My brain feels like a hunk of cold meat loaf, and it feels like my muscles have all been swapped with strips of boiled spinach. I know the rest of the guys feel the same.

When the phone rings, I don't think I have it in me to get up and go answer it. The kitchen seems about two hundred miles away.

But I go. I find some last, tiny, hidden pocket of

energy and drag myself across the house, thinking that it's probably my parents calling from the wedding they went to and that they'll start freaking out if I don't pick up.

"Hello?"

"Dan there?"

It's not my mom or dad. It's a kid. It sounds like—

"Edsley?" I say.

"Is Dan there?" he says again.

"Um, this is Ken," I tell him.

"Yeah, I know," Edsley tells me. "I called you, man. But I'm looking for Dan. Tell that guy I want my money back."

"Your money?"

"Tell him, Ken," says Edsley. "Tell him, or put him on the phone so I can tell him myself."

I pull the phone away from my face and call into the living room:

"Dan!"

"Unghhh?" he groans back.

"Edsley's on the phone. He says he wants his money back."

"Zero idea what he's talking about," says Dan.

Phone up to my face again, I tell Edsley:

"He says he doesn't have any of your money."

Edsley's silent.

"Mike?" I say.

"Yeah, well . . . ," he says, sounding frustrated with himself, but annoyed with *me* about it. "I guess I didn't actually *give* him any money, now that I think about it. But, whatever. Tell him that thing of his is a piece of trash."

"That thing of his?"

"Yeah," says Edsley. "The robot."

My stomach twists up into knots.

A beat later, Dan appears in the doorway. And it looks like he's in even worse shape than me. Like he's engaged in a battle to keep all his pizza and chocolate milk down in his stomach—and like he's about to lose.

Back into the phone, I say, "Mike, Dan told you not to open the box."

"I know," he says. "But that just got me curious. So I opened it up and put the thing together. And then the guy says he's hungry, so I make him a sandwich. Pretty nice of me, right? *I* thought so. But then he eats the thing all in one go and straightaway he asks for another.

 177

And I'm like, 'Make your own, man.' And that's when he swats at me. Swats at me and then storms right out the front door, straight down the street and out of sight."

"And now?" I ask him.

"Now? What do you mean *now*? How am *I* supposed to know where the stupid thing went?"

Acknowledgments

THANK YOU TO MOM AND DAD FOR ALL THE support and encouragement—I'm the luckiest kid in the world.

Thank you to my most excellent agent, Myrsini Stephanides, for believing in me and my work and for always going to bat for both.

Thank you to my thoughtful, sharp-eyed editor, Karen Nagel, for taking a chance on the EngiNerds and for doing all you did to make their story as good as it now is.

Thank you to Serge Seidlitz, Karin Paprocki, Chelsea Morgan, Randie Lipkin, Hilary Zarycky, Mara Anastas, and everyone else at Simon & Schuster/Aladdin who had a hand in making this book a reality.

And last but most of all, thank you to Danni Lerner for every big, little, and in-between-sized thing.

**Read on for a sneak peek at the
EngiNerds' next adventure:**

1.

THREE DAYS.

That's how long we've been looking for Edsley's robot.

Maybe that doesn't seem like that much time to you.

But each of those days contained twenty-four long hours.

That's seventy-two hours—or *4,320 minutes*—for that hungry, hungry robot to cause as much chaos, mayhem, and destruction as it pleased.

Over the course of those nearly forty-five hundred minutes, we've tried nearly everything to find the bot.

Some of our plans have been good. Some of them have been not-so-good. And a few, unfortunately, have been downright ridiculous.

And let me tell you—it hasn't been easy to keep the morale up and the momentum going among the guys. They went from determined to discouraged in about a day and a half, and now the majority of them are something even worse: distracted.

All of which has left me feeling desperate.

That's why I'm currently at the park with Edsley, twenty-six rotisserie chickens, and a pair of giant, industrial-strength fans. A part of me already knows this plan is one of our *most* not-so-good ones. But at least I'm doing *something*. At least I'm actively trying to find the robot before he blasts someone with a turd-missile or, I don't know, finds his way onto a computer and breaks the Internet.

Dan had a dentist appointment right after school today, and Edsley was the only other one of the guys I could convince to come with me—and only because I've been hammering into him every chance I get that it's all *his* fault the robot is on the loose and we've been spending so much time and energy looking for the thing in the first place.

Also, I promised to let him eat some of the chicken.

I turn to him.

"Mike!" I shout. "I said *some*, not *all*."

He holds his hands up, professing his innocence. His fingers are slick with chicken grease.

I shake my head and sigh.

"Will you just plug the fans in, man?"

Edsley reaches for my portable power pack. I wince,

thinking about how nasty he's going to leave the handle. I make a mental note to wipe it down with some disinfectant when I get home, then get the fans into position.

Here's the plan:

Step one—aim one fan one way, aim the other fan the other way.

Step two—set up half the rotisserie chickens in front of each fan and then turn those bad boys on full blast, sending the smell of the warm, oven-baked birds wafting across town.

Step three—wait for the missing robot's scent sensors to pick up on the irresistible aroma and come find us.

When he does, Edsley and I will douse the guy in water.

And then?

SQUAH-POOM!

Problem solved.

Because if there's one thing I'm sure of, it's that this robot has spent the past three days stuffing his stomach full of food and then squashing down all his meals and snacks into ultra-compact food-cubes. And when those puppies touch water, they expand, and rapidly enough to rip Mr. Dis-POS-al COM-*pleeet* apart.

"Ready?" I ask Edsley.

He places the last chicken on one of the overturned trash barrels we've got set up in front of the fans, then gives me a thumbs-up.

"*Please work . . . ,*" I mutter to myself.

I flip the switch on the power pack and the fans whir to life.

DO I REALLY NEED TO TELL YOU HOW THE
chicken-and-fan plan turned out?

Let's just say that the only butt-blaster that got doused in water was Edsley, after he "accidentally" sent a gust of some particularly foul gas in my direction.

That was after an hour and a half of sitting at the park with him, listening to those fans whir and wondering how many washes it'd be before my clothes no longer reeked of chicken, all while baking like birds in an oven our-selves under the uneasonably hot mid-May sun. I gave it another thirty minutes, then slumped home in defeat.

At lunch the next day, I don't even bother giving the rest of the EngiNerds an update.

I just move on.

"So," I say, opening a notebook to a blank page as I make my way up to the front of the room, "how'd the brainstorming go last night? Let's hear some new ideas about how to find this bot."

Crickets.

The guys just blink up at me.

The ones who are even looking at me, that is.

Some are completely tuned out, doing their own thing.

And I get it.

I do.

They're sick of banging their heads against the same problem and not making any progress.

I'm frustrated too.

But I'm also scared. Scared of what might happen if the robot shows up in the wrong place at the wrong time. And scared of what might happen if, after such an unfortunate incident, the bot gets traced back to Dan. Because he could get in some serious trouble. Maybe even *jail*-like trouble.

All of a sudden Edsley leaps up onto his feet.

His eyes are wide.

His mouth is hanging open.

"I've got it," he gasps. "I figured it out. We don't need to look for the robot anymore."